LUCK!

A New Musical

Book and Lyrics by
Mark Waldrop

Music by
Brad Ross

Based on a story by
Isaac Bashevis Singer

A SAMUEL FRENCH ACTING EDITION

SAMUEL FRENCH

FOUNDED 1830

NEW YORK HOLLYWOOD LONDON TORONTO

SAMUELFRENCH.COM

ISBN 978-0-573-69704-3   Printed in U.S.A.   #29118

IMPORTANT BILLING AND CREDIT REQUIREMENTS

LUCK!
A New Musical

Book and Lyrics by
Mark Waldrop

Music by
Brad Ross

Based on a story by
Isaac Bashevis Singer

LUCK! was performed in New York City as a staged reading in The York Theatre Company's Developmental Reading Series on July 9, 2009 with the following cast and crew:

MAZEL...Faith Prince

SHLIMAZEL....................................... Scott Davidson

TAM .... Stanley Bahorek

THE PRINCESS................................. Christina Sivrich

KAMSTAN .... John Herrera

THE KING......................................Gordon Stanley

GRILLIDA...Christine Pedi

ENSEMBLE .... Renee Bang Allen, Jane Blass, Jeff Essex
Stephanie Umoh, Darryl Winslow

Director – Stephen Nachamie
Musical Director – Brad Ross
Stage Manager – Alexis Qualls
Assistant Stage Manager – Stephanie Suski

CAST OF CHARACTERS

MAZEL	The personification of Good Luck [Female]
SHLIMAZEL	The personification of Bad Luck [Male]
TAM	A lad of humble birth
THE PRINCESS	A headstrong girl
KAMSTAN	The King's Prime Minister
THE KING	A quick tempered but benevolent ruler [Can play other roles]
GRILLIDA	The Princess' Nurse [Can play other roles]
ENSEMBLE	Plays all other roles including:
	PERIAPT, a henchman
	MERRYTHOUGHT, another henchman
	MERRY VILLAGERS
	LAUNDRY WOMAN
	ROYAL COACHMAN
	ROYAL BLACKSMITH
	ROYAL GROOM
	ROYAL GARDNER
	ROYAL CHEF
	THE ROYAL COURT
	FLYING SERPENTS
	A LIONESS
	DEMONS, IMPS, GOBLINS, etc.
	HANGSMAN

NOTE: *LUCK!* can be performed by a cast of 12, but the more the merrier.

ABOUT THE PRODUCTION:

There should be a primitive quality to the physical production. *LUCK!* is a folk tale and folk techniques should be used to tell it. Puppetry, shadows, masks, dance, trap-doors, flying: all these have a place here. The creativity that goes into showing a Lioness chasing Tam through the tall grass, a stage full of Demons or Flying Serpents, or any of the other "impossible" events detailed in the script should become a huge part of the shows' entertainment value. It is a story that presents many opportunities to engage the imagination of an audience in a way that is only possible in live theater.

MUSICAL NUMBERS

ACT 1

1 OVERTURE
2 LUCK! (Mazel, Shlimazel, Villagers)
3 HAIL! (Villagers)
4 NO ONE (Princess)
5 THIS ISN'T ME (Tam, Mazel, King)
6 WASTE NOT, WANT NOT (Grillida)
7 THE MAN CAN DO NO WRONG (Tam, Members of the Court)
8 WHO KNEW? (Mazel)
9 MORE THAN MEETS THE EYE (Kamstan)
10 HALF A WORLD AWAY (Tam, Princess)
11 TAM'S QUEST (Tam, Ensemble)
12 ONLY FEAR (Tam, Princess, Kamstan)

ACT 2

13 IT'S ME! (Mazel)
14 THE LUCKIEST MAN ALIVE (Tam, Kamstan)
15 WASTE NOT, WANT NOT Reprise (Grillida)
16 SHLIMAZEL'S WALTZ (Shlimazel, Demons)
17 GOODBYE (Princess)
18 INSIDE (Mazel, Tam)
19 LUCK! FINALE (Company)

ACT 1

Scene One

*(Music plays. We're on the outskirts of a folk-tale village. It is a market day in spring. Some **VILLAGERS** cross pushing a cart. A **MAN** passes with a cage of geese. A **WOMAN** trudges by with a basket of laundry. Curiously, none of them notices a beautiful female **SPIRIT** in a flowing gown who watches them with secret amusement. The laundry **WOMAN** trips, sending clothes flying. As she stoops, picking them up, the **SPIRIT** makes a gesture. There's a magical sound. The laundry **WOMAN** spies something in the dirt and cries out:)*

LAUNDRY WOMAN. A golden pfeffik! This is my lucky day!

*(She grabs the basket and skips off. The **SPIRIT**, pleased with herself, turns and vivaciously addresses the audience.)*

MAZEL. I did that. ...Hello. How are you? Hello. Nice to see you. I've visited so many of you before... But I know you've never seen me. Let me introduce myself. I'm called by many different names – Bona Fortuna. Buena Suerte. Bon Chance. But in this kingdom they call me...Mazel.

"LUCK!"

OH, I'M THE FABLED LADY LUCK,
ALWAYS SPOKEN WELL OF.
THE WORLD'S A FANCY BALL TO ME –
ONE THAT I'M THE BELLE OF.
I AM WOOED
AND PURSUED
EV'RYONE'S HEARD TELL OF

WONDERS THAT THE MAGIC OF MY TOUCH CAN BRING.
THERE'S NOT A SPIRIT ANYWHERE
QUITE SO INFLUENTIAL.
FOR ANYTHING TO TURN OUT WELL,
MAZEL IS ESSENTIAL.
SO YOU'LL UNDERSTAND ME WHEN I SING...

NOTHING IN ALL THE WORLD COMPARES TO LUCK!
LUCK IS A GIFT I'M FREE TO GIVE OR NOT.
LUCK IS THE DOORWAY TO SUCCESS
LUCK IS A GAMBLER'S DREAM
LUCK IS THE KEY TO HAPPINESS –
THAT'S WHY I REIGN SUPREME!
NOTHING IS UNPREDICTABLE AS LUCK!
LUCK CANNOT BE CONTROLLED,
THOUGH PEOPLE TRY.
WHEN MAZEL GIVES A SMILE
GOOD FORTUNE STAYS AWHILE.
I PAY MY LITTLE VISIT, THEN
I PACK ALL MY CHARMS AWAY
AND SAY GOODBYE.

*(***SCHLIMAZEL*** pops up through a trap door. His eyes and nose are red, his beard wild and unkempt. He's dressed in a tattered coat and a crushed hat.)*

SHLIMAZEL. Oh. Up here blowing your own horn. What a surprise!

MAZEL. Shlimazel! Must you always arrive so suddenly? What do you want?

SHLIMAZEL. Equal time.

MAZEL. Be my guest.

SHLIMAZEL.
SO TAKE A LOOK AT "LADY LUCK"
BASKING IN HER GLORY –
SHE'S TALKING LIKE ALL LUCK IS GOOD,
ONLY HALF THE STORY!
LET ME ADD, SOME LUCK'S BAD –
CHECK MY INVENTORY:
FAILURE, FLOP, FIASCO AND CATASTROPHE!
SHLIMAZEL ALWAYS PAYS A CALL.

WHEN YOU COURT DISASTER.
YOU WANT TO PLACE A LITTLE JINX?
COME AND SEE THE MASTER!
NO ONE'S HALF AS POWERFUL AS ME!

NOTHING'LL WRECK A LIFE LIKE ROTTEN LUCK.
LUCK, LIKE A STEAK, IS OFTEN PRETTY TOUGH.
LUCK IS A BOAT THAT SPRINGS A LEAK.
LUCK IS A RAINED OUT GAME.
LUCK IS A LIFETIME LOSING STREAK.
HEY, THAT'S MY CLAIM TO FAME!
NOTHING IS HARD TO SHAKE AS LOUSY LUCK!
LUCK LIKE A PESKY CINDER IN YOUR EYE.
SHLIMAZEL DOES HIS WORST;
YOUR FORTUNES ARE REVERSED.
THE WAY THE COOKIE CRUMBLES – THAT'S
THE KIND OF A BREAK THAT I
PERSONIFY!

(*Four* **VILLAGERS** *enter.*)

SHLIMAZEL. Let's look at a few examples…

MAZEL. Who are they?

SHLIMAZEL. Merry villagers! These folk tales are full of 'em.

MAZEL. They don't look very merry to me.

SHLIMAZEL. Well, folk tales aren't what they used to be.

MAZEL. Why the long faces?

SHLIMAZEL. I hate to brag, but…listen…

VILLAGERS. (*variously*)

THAT DAMNED OLD SHLIMAZEL. HE GAVE ME A SHOVE
FLAT BROKE.
MENOPAUSAL,
IN THE DOGHOUSE,
OUT OF LOVE…OH,
PLEASE WHERE ARE YOU, MAZEL?
GET ME OUT OF THIS!
MY LIFE'S
UGLY FLAWS'LL
BE CORRECTED
BY YOUR KISS!

MAZEL. You see Shlimazel? The more you exert yourself, the more they cry for me! Oh, they want me so!

VILLAGERS.
RANT, RAVE,
RAISE THE RAFTERS
LAUGH OR CRY ABOUT IT...
HOW DULL LIFE WOULD BE WITHOUT IT...

MAZEL, SHLIMAZEL, VILLAGERS.
NOTHING'LL MAKE A MAN IMMUNE TO LUCK.
LUCK IS A FACTOR THAT YOU CANNOT PLAN.
LUCK IS A THING TO FLUCTUATE;
LUCK DISAPPEARS, AND THEN
LUCK IN A FLASH'LL CHANGE YOUR FATE –
THEN CHANGE IT BACK AGAIN!
NOTHING'LL TURN LIFE UPSIDE DOWN LIKE LUCK. (LUCK!)
LUCK THAT'LL LAY YOU LOW OR TAKE YOU HIGH!

MAZEL.
WHEN MAZEL SAYS HELLO
HER BLESSING SHE'LL BESTOW.

SHLIMAZEL.
THEN UP SHLIMAZEL POPS
AND TUMBLING DOWN YOUR FORTUNES GO-OH!

MAZEL.
YOU TAKE A RISK; IT TURNS OUT WELL!

SHLIMAZEL.
YOU HAVE A SURE THING SHOT TO HELL!

ALL.
SAY WHAT YOU WILL, THERE'S NO DENYING
LUCK IS WHY!
LUCK!

(**VILLAGERS** *exit.* **MAZEL** *and* **SHLIMAZEL** *remain.*)

MAZEL. Goodbye, Merry Villagers. I guess that's the last we'll see of them.

SHLIMAZEL. Oh, they'll be back. In this kind of story they keep turning up like a bad penny.

MAZEL. Those Merry Villagers are nice. They all love *me*.

SHLIMAZEL. Mazel. You're such a tease.

MAZEL. A *what!!?*

SHLIMAZEL. A tease! A flirt. You dilly here, you dally there – then it's on to the next! Me, I latch on to some poor schnook and stick like glue.

MAZEL. *(dubiously)* I could stick with one person – if I wanted to.

SHLIMAZEL. You? Forget it. It's not your nature.

MAZEL. I could!

SHLIMAZEL. You want to bet?

MAZEL. Fine.

SHLIMAZEL. What are the terms?

MAZEL. *(thinking quickly)* All right… I will go to the poorest hut in this village and bring happiness to whoever lives there. I will remain with that person for an entire *year.*

SHLIMAZEL. This I gotta see.

MAZEL. The moment the year is at an end, he's yours for one year.

SHLIMAZEL. Fine. I'll take the year. But you know how much of it I'll need to undo ALL you've done? One second!

MAZEL. You're crazy.

SHLIMAZEL. If I do it, then *I* win! And when I do, you will give me…a barrel of the Wine of Forgetfulness.

MAZEL. Fine! And if you lose, you keep your nose out of my business for fifty years. Agreed?

SHLIMAZEL. Agreed.

MAZEL. It's a bet!

(They shake on it.)

SHLIMAZEL. So bring on the poorest hut in the village…

Scene Two – Outside Tam's Hut

(A tumbledown hovel comes into view. It's made of dirty, primitive bricks. The thatch roof has fallen in. The single window is broken. On a low stoop in a doorway sits a forlorn young man – **TAM** *– dressed in filthy rags.)*

SHLIMAZEL. Wow! Talk about your fixer upper!

MAZEL. Don't judge a person by his house.

SHLIMAZEL. What house? I'm talking about the kid.

MAZEL. Young man, who are you?

TAM. My name is Tam.

SHLIMAZEL. Hey! Humans cannot see or hear us. How are you doing that?

MAZEL. Just a little trick. He thinks he's talking to himself.

TAM. Oh great. Now I'm talking to myself. What next?

(A brick falls onto **TAM** *'s head – woodblock. SFX.)*

TAM. *(rubbing his head)* Ow!

MAZEL. How did you come to be so down and out?

TAM. I'm the unlucky son of an unlucky son of an unlucky man. *(Another brick falls – woodblock SFX. The business is repeated.)* Ow!

SHLIMAZEL. Good background. *(to* **TAM***)* Go on...

TAM. My grandfather went into the forest to look for food. On his way home with a basket of mushrooms, he was bitten by a poisonous snake.

MAZEL. And your father?

TAM. He died from eating the mushrooms. *(Another brick falls. Woodblock SFX.)* Ow! Stupid bricks.

(He tosses the brick over his shoulder. It hits the wall, and the entire house collapses. **TAM***, seated now in front of the pile of rubble, glances over his shoulder.)*

Oh great – just when I got the mortgage paid off.

SHLIMAZEL. I love this kid. A perfect subject. Agreed?

MAZEL. Agreed!

SHLIMAZEL. Your year starts…now!

> (**MAZEL** *makes a magical gesture. There is a distant bugle call. The* **VILLAGERS** *rush on.*)

SHLIMAZEL. I told you they'd be back.

VILLAGER #1. Tam! Tam! Get up! Make yourself scarce! The King and his royal party are about to pass along this road!

VILLAGER #2. They're on their way home from a neighboring kingdom.

VILLAGER #3. We can't let them see you! You'll disgrace the entire village! Quick! Hide!

> (*We hear the horn again, closer now, accompanied by hoof beats.*)

VILLAGER #4. Hurry! Hurry! They're almost here!

> (**TAM** *is pushed from view. The* **VILLAGERS** *look expectantly to the wings.*)

"HAIL"

VILLAGERS.

> HIP-HIP HURRAH!
> LIFT UP YOUR VOICE AND SING.
>
> HAIL TO HIS MAJESTY!
> OUR NOBLE KING!
>
> EV'RYBODY'S HAPPY
> IN HIS DOMAIN.
> THOUGH HE CAN BE A RE-AL
> ROYAL PAIN!
>
> GIVE A HUZZAH
> TO OUR BELOVED PRINCESS!
> STILL NEVER MARRIED
> AND A TOTAL MESS!
>
> THEY LOOK DOWN UPON US
> FROM THRONES ON HIGH!
> SO HAIL AND FAREWELL TO THEM!
> (HAIL AND FAREWELL TO THEM!)

*(The **VILLAGERS** doff their hats and wave as the royal carriage crosses. Inside the carriage we glimpse the **KING** and the **PRINCESS**.)*

VILLAGERS. *(cont.)*
WAVE
AS
THEY
RIDE
BY....

*(The carriage has just passed into the wings when there is a deafening crash. The **VILLAGERS** react in horror. One of the carriage's ornate wheels rolls back across the stage. **MAZEL** stops it.)*

MAZEL. Oh, I'm good. I'm very good.

SHLIMAZEL. Since when is losing a wheel good luck?

MAZEL. A misfortune there may yield an opportunity here. Wait and see.

*(The **VILLAGERS** start off toward the crash site, then move back, bowing and curtsying as the **KING** and **PRINCESS** enter. The **PRINCESS** carries a book. A **COACHMAN** runs across and examines the wheel. It breaks in half.)*

COACHMAN. *(bone-headedly stating the obvious)* Your majesty, this wheel is broken.

KING. Well, jack the carriage up and put on the spare!

COACHMAN. Right away, Your Majesty. You! Merry Villagers! Don't stand there gawking. Help us lift the royal carriage from that ditch!

*(The **VILLAGERS** exit. **TAM** lags behind. The **COACHMAN** points to **TAM**.)*

You!

*(The **COACHMAN** indicates with a snap of his fingers that **TAM** is to drop to all fours. **TAM** obeys. The **COACHMAN** removes his cloak and covers **TAM** with it. The **KING** and **PRINCESS** sit on **TAM** without taking special notice – clearly this is the kind of treatment to which*

they are accustomed. Immediately, the **PRINCESS** *buries her nose in her book. The* **COACHMAN** *exits. The* **KING** *regards the pile of rubble that used to be Tam's house.)*

KING. Look at this! My kingdom is in shambles! I don't know what else could go wrong! This entire journey has been a disaster! The grandest ball we've been to yet! Two hundred oxen roasted on spits. Printed matchbooks. They went all out! ...Look at me when I'm talking to you!

PRINCESS. *(lowering the book)* But Father, the prince made me feel nothing! Not a twinge. Not a pang.

KING. He was the last eligible prince! We can't wait for the next crop – you'll be too old!

PRINCESS. Father, you're a man. You just don't understand!

KING. If your mother were alive, she'd tell you the same thing.

PRINCESS. No! She'd tell me to marry for love.

KING. And what do you know about love?

PRINCESS. I may not have any first-hand experience – but I've been a very good student...

"NO ONE"

PRINCESS.

I'VE HEARD ALL THE BALLADS.
I'VE READ ALL THE VERSES.
I'VE BLUSHED OVER STORIES
RECITED BY NURSES.
I KNOW THAT TRUE LOVE
MUST PRODUCE AN EFFECT.
AND I'VE MET MANY MEN,
BUT I'M SAD TO REPORT
NOT A ONE CAUSED A STIR
OF THE PHYSICAL SORT
THAT MY RESEARCH LEADS ME TO EXPECT:

NO ONE MAKES MY SKIN GO CRIMSON.
NO ONE MAKES MY BLOOD CONGEAL.
NO ONE BRINGS ABOUT THE TORMENT
A GIRL IN LOVE SHOULD FEEL.

(She rises and moves about.)

PRINCESS. *(cont.)*

> JUST ONCE CAN'T I HAVE A SPASM?
> CAN'T I LOSE MY SANITY?
> MY FINE, FLOURISHING STATE
> CAN ONLY INDICATE
> THERE'S NO ONE,
> NO ONE FOR ME!
>
> ALL I WANT IS WHAT A GIRL DESERVES:
> SOME BASIC PALPITATIONS AND A CASE OF SHATTERED
>   NERVES!
>
> WHERE'S THE PRINCE TO FAN MY PASSION
> TILL I BREAK INTO A RASH, AND
> I AM FAINTING AT THE MENTION OF HIS NAME?
> IS IT TOO MUCH TO BE WISHIN'
> FOR A MYSTERY CONDITION
> WHERE THE DOCTORS ALL CONCUR A MAN'S TO BLAME?
> WHO WILL STEAL AWAY MY APPETITE?
> WHO WILL MAKE ME PITCH AND MOAN AND SHIVER
>   THROUGH THE SLEEPLESS NIGHT?
>
> NO ONE! I AM UNAFFLICTED!
> NO FUN BEING SYMPTOM FREE!

*(Returning to the **KING**'s side, sitting on **TAM**.)*

> WILL THERE COME ONE WHO WILL BE
> SOMEONE, SOMEONE...?

*(She looks around – the silence is her answer. In frustration she pounds her fist into **TAM**'s back.)*

TAM. *(from under the cloak)* Ow.

PRINCESS.

> NO ONE FOR ME!

*(End of number; applause. **MAZEL** and **SCHLIMAZEL** watch from the sidelines. The **PRINCESS** resumes reading.)*

SHLIMAZEL. Let me guess...

MAZEL. And why shouldn't she find the one she's looking for right under her nose? Or her...

SHLIMAZEL. So – you're going to marry him off to a princess? How original!

MAZEL. Shh! The Princess is more obtuse than I might have wished. No matter. There's more than one shortcut to success.

(She pulls a golden blowpipe from her sleeve and loads it with a bean retrieved from her décolletage. The **COACHMAN** *returns with the* **VILLAGERS**, *who are pushing the royal coach, now minus a wheel.)*

COACHMAN. *(cringing)* Your Majesty, a thousand pardons – but the spare is broken, too.

KING. *(jumping up)* This is the limit! How much do I have to put up with in one day? *(to the* **COACHMAN***)* Incompetence! *(to the* **PRINCESS***)* Insubordination! *(to the* **VILLAGERS***)* Which one of you can fix that wheel and get us rolling again? Well? A gold coin for anyone who can repair it!

*(***MAZEL** *shoots the bean at* **TAM**, *who leaps up, causing the* **PRINCESS** *to stand and drop her book..)*

TAM. Ow! I can...Your Highness...

(The **VILLAGERS** *gasp.)*

KING. Is this the best the village has to offer? This filthy scarecrow? No wonder the tax base is declining! Well?

*(***TAM** *has focused on the* **PRINCESS** *and is momentarily transfixed.* **MAZEL** *whispers into his ear.)*

MAZEL. Yes, the Princess is very beautiful. But one thing at a time. Focus on the task at hand.

KING. I warn you, boy: trifle with me I'll deal harshly with you – and your village! If you think you can fix this wheel then do it – and do it quickly!

*(***MAZEL** *gives* **TAM** *a whack on the back.)*

TAM. Right away, Your Majesty!

(Bewildered, but realizing it's too late to back out, **TAM** *moves to the wheel and sets to work.)*

"*THIS ISN'T ME*"

TAM.

> THIS ISN'T ME
> WHO'S DOING THIS?
> IT'S WEIRD –
> WHO VOLUNTEERED ME?
> I NEVER DID,
> I NEVER WOULD, I NEVER COULD.
> THIS CANNOT BE REAL.
> THIS ISN'T ME
> WHAT'S HAPPENING?
> OH NO –
> I'M GONNA THROW UP.
> CAN I SURVIVE
> COME OUT ALIVE?
> ACTUALLY, I'VE
> NEVER FIXED A WHEEL!

> I've never even *owned* anything with a wheel. Not a cart or a wagon or…

MAZEL.

> BREATHE.
> LEAVE IT TO ME.
> SMILE AND KEEP ON MOVING.
> LIFE WILL BE IMPROVING FOR YOU…

TAM.

> OH MY GOD I'M PANIC-STRICKEN
> FLAPPING LIKE A HEADLESS CHICKEN!

> What am I gonna do?! I have no tools! I have no hammer!

MAZEL. Tam, calm down. If you don't have a hammer, why not try a brick?

TAM. *(hysterical)* Where am I going to get a brick?!

MAZEL. See that pile of rubble that used to be your hut? Think of it as a home supply center.

TAM. *(as if it's a new thought)* Maybe I'll try a brick. Here's one, and…Oh, look! Here's a nail. Oh, look! It's a piece of metal gutter! This looks like it could bend around and…Oh, look! A perfect fit!

(Bang-Bang-Bang, he secures the nail with the brick.)

TAM. *(cont.)* Good as new! Now I'll just slip it on the axle, and…Hmm. It's not turning. I seem to need some lubricant…

(Suddenly he sneezes, covering his mouth and nose with his hand. He looks into his palm, considers for a moment, then…)

Okay!

(He sets about lubricating the axle.)

SHLIMAZEL. Hah! He hasn't even secured that wheel! You know perfectly well, the minute that carriage rolls it could fall off!

MAZEL. It could. But as Luck would have it, it will stay on! This boy's a fast learner. He came up with that sneezing business all by himself.

TAM. *(stepping back from his handiwork)* All done!

*(The **VILLAGERS** cheer.)*

MAZEL.

THE WHEEL OF FORTUNE, HAVING SPUN,
FORETELLS A JOURNEY SOON BEGUN!

*(The **KING** presents **TAM** with the gold piece.)*

KING.

YOUNG MAN, A CRAFTSMAN OF YOUR SORT
WOULD BE A CREDIT TO MY COURT!
THE WHEEL IS FIXED; WE'RE SET TO RIDE.
WOULD YOU CARE TO STEP INSIDE?

TAM. *(triumphantly)*

THIS ISN'T ME
IT'S SOMEBODY
SECURE,
FULL OF BRAVURA.
I NEVER THOUGHT,
I NEVER DREAMED,
I NEVER HOPED
SUCH EVENTS COULD BE.
MY HOME'S A WRECK,
WHY SHOULD I STAY?

MAZEL.

> NOW OFF YOU GO,
> YOU'RE ON YOUR WAY!

TAM.

> NOW SEEMS THE PERFECT DAY TO PAY A VISIT –
> BUT
> THIS ISN'T RIGHT,
> THIS ISN'T REAL,
> THIS ISN'T ME...

ALL.

> OR IS IT?

> (**TAM** *climbs into the carriage with the* **KING** *and* **PRIN-CESS** *and off they ride.*)

Scene Three – Interior of the Royal Palace

(At a small table **KAMSTAN***, the* **KING***'s prime minister, is finishing what looks to have been a lavish meal. Two tall bundles of books are downstage.* **MERRYTHOUGHT***,* **KAMSTAN***'s cohort, stands reading aloud from one of them.)*

MERRYTHOUGHT. "...And as the swarthy Woodcutter crushed her in his arms, the disguise slipped from his chiseled torso. There it was! The royal birthmark! The Princess felt her heart swell to bursting with joy! At last! The gypsy's prediction had come true...!"

KAMSTAN. *(doing a spit-take with his wine, laughing)* Stop! Stop! It's perfect! Oh, it's expensive to keep those hacks grinding out this drivel – but it's worth it! Now go! I want these romances waiting in the Princess' chamber when she returns!

MERRYTHOUGHT. Right away, your slyness.

*(***MERRYTHOUGHT*** gathers up the books and exits as* **PERIAPT***, another henchman, rushes in and bows before* **KAMSTAN***)*

PERIAPT. Your grace.

KAMSTAN. Well, Periapt – what news?

PERIAPT. Your grace, the royal party has been delayed in the village. I returned by another road, unobserved.

KAMSTAN. And? The ball?

PERIAPT. *(gleefully)* A complete washout!

KAMSTAN. The match failed to ignite?

PERIAPT. Not a spark!

KAMSTAN. Excellent! As long as the Princess stays unwed, if the King dies, by law the kingdom passes to me. It's just a matter of time!

PERIAPT. *(knocking on the table)* If nothing goes wrong.

KAMSTAN. Fool! Nothing will go wrong – because I leave nothing to chance! Who else would take pains to fill the Princess' mind with romantic claptrap? Who else

would drill a series of concealed holes beside the
King's bed to create an unhealthy draft? Who else
would send you to the next kingdom disguised as an
traveling barber for the express purpose of giving the
prince a bad haircut? Genius is in the details!

*(**GRILLIDA**, the **PRINCESS**' nurse, rushes in.)*

GRILLIDA. Your grace, the royal carriage just pulled up!
There's a young man with them! I've had my fingers
crossed for three days. Perhaps my lady has found a
prince to please her at last!

KAMSTAN. We can only hope.

GRILLIDA. Here they come now!

*(The **KING** and **PRINCESS** enter with **TAM**, who is flipping the gold piece and slapping it against the back of his
hand repeatedly. The **PRINCESS** carries a fading nosegay
of purple roses and a large spotted balloon. **MAZEL** follows at a discreet distance, invisible to all. **KAMSTAN**
makes a low bow. **GRILLIDA** curtsies. **MERRYTHOUGHT**
returns. He and **PERIAPT** stand to one side.)*

KAMSTAN. Your majesty! I trust this journey yielded success
at last?

KING. It couldn't have been worse! The Princess took one
look at the Prince and didn't stop laughing for the rest
of the evening.

PRINCESS. It was his hair…

*(Unseen by the others **KAMSTAN** and **PERIAPT** exchange
a "thumbs-up.")*

KING. We're clean out of candidates – unless a miracle lit-
erally lands on our doorstep…

KAMSTAN. *(eyeing **TAM** distastefully)* And what is this?

KING. Oh. This is a clever lad from the village. He fixed the
royal carriage.

KAMSTAN. And why is he flipping that coin?

KING. It's a talent he discovered in the carriage! He has
called heads or tails correctly…how many times?

TAM. Two hundred and fourteen, Your Majesty.

(TAM flips again. KAMSTAN draws close to watch.)

KING. Call it!

TAM. Heads.

(Heads it is.)

KING. *(vastly amused)* Remarkable, isn't it? Kamstan, I want you to clean this boy up and put him to work in the royal smithy.

KAMSTAN. At once, Your Majesty. Periapt, Merrythought – see to it.

(PERIAPT and MERRYTHOUGHT exit with TAM, followed by MAZEL. The KING crosses to the PRINCESS and GRILLIDA.)

KING. Lady Grillida. The Princess has no mother to instruct her. You were brought on as her nurse to provide a woman's guidance. Talk some sense into her!

GRILLIDA. *(curtsying)* I'll do my best, Your Majesty.

(The KING crosses to KAMSTAN.)

KING. I suppose we have affairs of state to catch up on?

KAMSTAN. Nothing that can't wait. You look weary from the trip. Might I suggest an invigorating ice-bath – followed by a long nap?

(They exit. GRILLIDA seats herself at the table and samples the leftovers. The PRINCESS sits opposite her.)

GRILLIDA. So tell me everything! This prince was not suitable? Surely a haircut would grow out, could be fixed... A larger crown, perhaps...

PRINCESS. Grillida, he was unbearable! Three times he told me the same story about his prowess at hunting the wild boar. He gave me these...

(The PRINCESS tosses the nosegay onto the table.)

GRILLIDA. Purple roses! Do you not want them?

PRINCESS. Take them, they're yours.

GRILLIDA. Thank you, my lady. *(She turns her attention to the balloon.)* And may I ask, what is that?

PRINCESS. That prince made me take it. The entire ball-room was decorated with them.

*(**GRILLIDA** holds it aloft.)*

GRILLIDA. Such a light airy thing! What is it?

PRINCESS. The bladder of a wild boar.

*(The bladder pops in **GRILLIDA**'s hands, startling them both. **GRILLIDA** regards the limp remains.)*

GRILLIDA. I'll keep this too.

(She drops the roses and the popped bladder into her satchel.)

PRINCESS. Ewwww.

GRILLIDA. You never know when these things will come in handy for a potion or a poultice.

"WASTE NOT, WANT NOT"

GRILLIDA.

A PUNCTURED BLADDER
MAY BE TRASH TO YOU –
BUT WHO KNOWS WHAT ITS WORTH MAY TRULY BE?
IT MIGHT FORM A GASKET
OR PATCH AN OLD BASKET
OR PROVE TO BE MEDICINAL WHEN BREWED FOR TEA...

I'LL STASH IT AWAY JUST IN CASE...
AND PLEASE WIPE THAT LOOK OFF YOUR FACE!

WASTE NOT, WANT NOT
THAT'S MY CREED
WHO CAN SAY WHEN I MIGHT NEED
THAT SNIP OF HAIR
CHIP OF SOAP
DRIP OF OIL
SCRAP OF ROPE?

WASTE NOT, WANT NOT
THAT'S MY PLAN

SO I RAID THE GARBAGE CAN!
WITH SOME CREATIVE JUICE
EVEN JUNK
HAS ITS USE.

PRINCESS. Yes, I know. You're a packrat.

GRILLIDA.

ONCE YOU'VE GOT IT, KEEP IT HANDY
THERE'S NO NEED TO FUSS OR FUTZ
STACK YOUR STOCKPILE UP AND GUARD IT
LIKE A SQUIRREL GUARDS HIS NUTS.

WASTE NOT, WANT NOT
THAT'S MY STYLE
COMBING THROUGH THE RUBBISH PILE.
NEVER THROW THOSE ODDS AND ENDS AWAY!
IT'S MORE CLEVER TO SAVE WHATEVER IT IS FOR A RAINY
DAY!

(MUSIC continues under.)

PRINCESS. Is that philosophy supposed to be news to me? Grillida, you haven't changed that tune since I was a little girl.

*(**GRILLIDA** tucks into some **KAMSTAN**'s leftover dinner.)*

GRILLIDA. Exactly. Why should I let a perfectly good tune go to waste? Now, where were we…? The Prince!

PRINCESS. That topic is closed.

GRILLIDA. *(talking with her mouth full)* But, your highness, if you are ever to rule, the law is clear; you need a husband. I was sure this prince would be the one! Ever since you left I hopped over every crack in the courtyard. I kept a knotted string under your pillow…

(As she talks she knocks over a saltshaker and tosses some over her shoulder.)

PRINCESS. My poor superstitious Grillida! You can't manufacture good luck for me. Anyway, love is more than luck.

*(**PERIAPT** and **MERRYTHOUGHT** march **TAM** by in the background, looking like he's been hosed down.)*

GRILLIDA. And what about that lad you brought from the village?

PRINCESS. Just a local boy Father took a shine to.

GRILLIDA. And could he not be a nobleman under an enchantment? An heir to a kingdom traveling in disguise?

PRINCESS. Him? Don't be ridiculous!

GRILLIDA.

WASTE NOT, WANT NOT
I'D ADVISE
NOTICE WHAT'S BEFORE YOUR EYES
WHY UNDERESTIMATE
WHAT COULD BE
SOMETHING GREAT?

FIRST IMPRESSIONS MAY MISLEAD YOU
ALWAYS TAKE A SECOND GLANCE
SOMEONE DREADFUL COULD BE PERFECT
IN A DIFFERENT CIRCUMSTANCE.

WASTE NOT, WANT NOT
GOOD CAN HIDE
IN WHAT MIGHT BE TOSSED ASIDE
WIPE AWAY THE TARNISH AND THE GRIME
AND YOU COULD BRING TO LIGHT AN ITEM YOU'RE GOING
TO NEED SOMETIME.

Scene Four – The Royal Smithy and Various Locations Around the Palace

(An anvil, a furnace, various carriages and coaches. **TAM** *is hammering a red-hot horse shoe. The* **BLACK-SMITH** *stands to one side with the* **COACHMAN** *and the* **GROOM,** *examining a coach which is up on blocks.* **MAZEL** *and* **SHLIMAZEL** *are perched above, observing.)*

SHLIMAZEL. Two weeks into the bet, and the poor kid is down here in the bowels of the palace drenched in sweat. You call this good luck? He's working like a dog!

MAZEL. I know you may not understand this, Schlimazel, but good luck is all *about* hard work.

SHLIMAZEL. Yeah? Well, he can have it.

MAZEL. He does. And he's making the most of it.

*(***GRILLIDA*** *enters as if she's a spy on a secret mission. The* **BLACKSMITH** *steps out to greet her. He is a rough looking man with a wooden leg, a hook for a hand and an eye patch.)*

BLACKSMITH. And what brings your ladyship to our lowly quarters?

GRILLIDA. I need a lucky horse shoe – one that will help the Princess find a suitable husband.

BLACKSMITH. *(mockingly adopting her tone)* Does the Princess actually think a horseshoe has that kind of power?

GRILLIDA. No. But I do. And she needs all the help she can get.

BLACKSMITH. My lady, if horseshoes brought good luck, wouldn't *I* – a blacksmith – be the luckiest man in the kingdom? And look at me*! (He indicates the wooden leg, the hook, the eye patch. He holds out a horseshoe.)* Here. Take this and be quick about it.

GRILLIDA. No! You have it upside down! All the luck has run out the ends!

BLACKSMITH. Take it or leave it! I have work to do.

(He returns to work. **GRILLIDA** *starts to exit.* **TAM** *beckons her over.)*

TAM. Psst. Your ladyship! Please take this to the Princess with my compliments.

(Smiling, he hands her a horseshoe with the ends pointing up. She accepts it and rushes off. **TAM** *returns to work.)*

SHLIMAZEL. Hah! People are such idiots. As if a horseshoe had magical powers!

MAZEL. Tam gave it with a kind heart. Even if the horseshoe is worthless, the gesture might prove lucky.

BLACKSMITH. Tam! The King paid a fortune for this fancy foreign coach and it's in the shop more than it's on the road. See what you can do.

TAM. Right away, sir!

(He slides under the coach and starts hammering. The **BLACKSMITH, GROOM,** *and* **COACHMAN** *look on.)*

COACHMAN. That new lad is a hard worker.

BLACKSMITH. And skillful, too. He's like nothing I've ever seen before!

"THE MAN CAN DO NO WRONG"

BLACKSMITH.

HE CAN MEND A CARRIAGE THAT IS CRACKED BEYOND
    REPAIR
QUICKER THAN A FLASH
IT'S AS GOOD AS NEW.
HE CAN FIX A NICK LIKE IT WAS NEVER EVEN THERE –
ANY JOB YOU'VE GOT, HE'LL DO!

COACHMAN.

HE CAN GREASE AN AXLE THAT HAS ALWAYS HAD A
    SQUEAK.
TAKE A LITTLE SPIN,
YOU WON'T HEAR A SOUND.

TAM.

OH, IT'S NORTHING REALLY, JUST A MATTER OF TECHNIQUE.
(AND THE LUCKY STREAK I'VE FOUND!)

IT'S AS THOUGH MY FUTURE CAME AND SLAPPED ME ON
    THE BACK!
ONCE I WAS A KNUCKLEHEAD BUT NOW I HAVE A KNACK!

BLACKSMITH.

ANYTHING HE SETS ABOUT,
HE SEES IT OUT WITH STYLE!

GROOM.

LIVELY AND ALERT.

COACHMAN.

NOT AFRAID OF DIRT.

BLACKSMITH.

IF YOU TWO WERE MORE LIKE HIM –
I HAVE TO SAY, IT WOULDN'T HURT.

BLACKSMITH, COACHMAN, GROOM.

HIS SKILL HE'LL SHARE WITH ONE AND ALL.
JUST ASK! NO TASK TOO GREAT OR SMALL.
HE'S ON THE JOB AND ON THE BALL.
THE MAN CAN DO NO WRONG!

HE TACKLES WORK WITH ZEAL AND ZEST.
HE'S MORE THAN UP TO ANY TEST.
RESULTS ARE IN, AND THEY SUGGEST:
THE MAN CAN DO NO WRONG!

(The **BLACKSMITH, COACHMAN,** *and* **GROOM** *exit
with the forge. A GARDEN is revealed. In the background* **TAM** *rolls on a wheelbarrow and sets out plants.
Everything he touches bursts into bloom. The* **ROYAL
GARDNER** *appears.)*

GARDNER. Two months Tam has been working as a greens
man, and he's already tripled crop yield, invented a
new system of irrigation, and redesigned the topiary
display!

SHOW THE MAN A VACANT LOT, HE'LL MAKE A GARDEN
    THRIVE:
RUTABAGA, LEEK, APRICOT AND PLUM!
TWENTY YEARS IVE BEEN A GARDENER, AND I TELL YOU, I'VE
NEVER SEEN A GREENER THUMB!

*(**GRILLIDA** enters.)*

GRILLIDA. Young man...Oh, hello. It's you again. Have you come across any four leaf clovers in this garden?

TAM. Why, no. I haven't been looking for... Oh! Here's one right here.

(Effortlessly, **TAM** *spots a four leaf clover and presents it to* **GRILLIDA.** *)*

GRILLIDA. Why, thank you...um...

TAM. Tam!

GRILLIDA. Thank you, Tam!

*(***GRILLIDA** *curtsies and both exit. The garden is replaced by a Kitchen. The* **ROYAL CHEF** *enters.)*

CHEF. Two months in the kitchen and he's developed the pastry bag, the egg timer, and a complete line of non-stick cookware!

(As the **CHEF** *sings,* **TAM** *reappears immediately dressed as a cook. With some clever sleight of hand he turns some highly unlikely ingredients into a dazzling confection.)*

RECIPES, HE DOESN'T NEED – HE LIKES TO IMPROVISE:
HUMMINGBIRD ON TOAST, ROASTED WILDEBEEST,
SAVORIES TO TEASE THE TONGUE AND TITILLATE THE EYES!
HE CAN MAKE A MEAL A FEAST!

*(***GRILLIDA** *enters.)*

GRILLIDA. Hello, Tam. I wanted to compliment you on the rabbit stew...

*(***TAM** *offers her a rabbit's foot.)*

TAM. My lady, might you be needing this?

GRILLIDA. A rabbit's foot! Oh, you're too kind. The Princess will be most appreciative.

(She curtsies and exits. The kitchen disappears. **TAM** *is surrounded by a group of* **LEARNED MEN** *in dark cloaks.)*

LEARNED MEN.

IN A TOUGH DEBATE HE'S ALWAYS EAGER TO ENGAGE.
HE DISPLAYS THE WISDOM OF A SCHOLAR TWICE HIS AGE.
MATTERS CONTRADICTORY HE CLARIFIES WITH EASE.

(A bevy of **COURT LADIES** *dressed in party finery burst through, pulling* **TAM** *with them.* **TAM** *is now wearing a smart and expensive ensemble. Clearly, his status is improving.)*

LADIES.

CANDY FOR THE EYES!
WHAT A PAIR OF THIGHS!
ANYONE CAN PLAINLY SEE
THE REASON HE IS ON THE RISE!
HIS REPARTEE IS GLORIOUS.
HIS JOKES ARE ALL UPROARIOUS.
WITH LADIES HE'S NOTORIOUS.
THE MAN CAN DO NO WRONG.

MAZEL. Is it me, or does this Royal Court look a lot like the Merry Villagers?

SHLIMAZEL. Listen, on this budget, there's gonna be some overlap.

ALL.

ALL ACROSS THE KINGDOM PEOPLE SING ABOUT HIS DEEDS!
HILL AND VALLEY ECHO HIS ACCLAIM!
EV'RY DAY THE STORIES SEEM TO MULTIPLY LIKE WEEDS,
EV'RYONE'S DELIGHTED BY HIS FAME!
(EXCUSE OUR GUSHING ON,
BUT GOD, THE GUY'S A PARAGON!)

HIS RISE HAS BEEN UPSTOPPABLE! (WE ALL PRIZE HIM!)
HIS RECORD IS UNTOPPABLE! (IDOLIZE HIM!)
HE'S ALWAYS RIGHT,
GALLANT, POLITE,
HE'S HANDSOME, BRIGHT
AND STRONG!
IT'S TRUE THE MAN CAN DO NO WRONG!

*(***TAM** *is held aloft on the* **COURT***'s shoulders.* **TAM** *is lit in the final tableau, as are* **MAZEL** *and the* **PRINCESS***.)*

Scene Five – The Terrace

(**SHLIMAZEL** *enters and pulls* **MAZEL** *downstage as the tableau breaks and the scene shifts.*)

SCHLIMAZEL. Wow. You're really going to town with this kid.

MAZEL. It's fun. And where have you been?

SCHLIMAZEL. Oh, just out and about. Why should I hang around here?

MAZEL. Shh! Look...

(*They draw to one side as the* **PRINCESS** *enters with* **TAM.** *Music plays softly under.*)

PRINCESS. So much has happened to you since we first met. The court talks of no one else. I've been wanting to speak with you.

TAM. And I have so much I've wanted to tell you. But... Let me see something first.

(*He takes the coin from his pocket and flips it.* **TAM** *smiles and pockets the coin.*)

PRINCESS. Is your luck still holding?

TAM. Yes. (*An awkward moment. Then...*) From up here the village looks so tiny.

PRINCESS. Tam, that village *is* tiny. It's even tiny up close. Do you miss it?

TAM. Not for a second. Why, when I lived there I was as wretched a human being as you could ever see! But then my destiny turned around! And do you know what happened at the very moment my life changed forever? I saw you!

(*The* **PRINCESS** *gives a little gasp and her hand goes to her mouth. Quickly she pulls it back and glances at her finger.*)

PRINCESS. Oh!

(*She tips her head back.*)

TAM. Princess, what's wrong?

PRINCESS. Nothing. A nose bleed.

TAM. Here. Take my handkerchief.

(He helps her towards a bench, and they sit.)

PRINCESS. I've never felt quite like this before. Keep talking, Tam. Tell me what's in your heart.

(Lights shift. **MAZEL** *and* **SHLIMAZEL** *are revealed again, observing.)*

MAZEL. *(fondly)* See how Tam's fortunes are turning? Look.

SHLIMAZEL. I'm not really one for all this mushy stuff. *After* the wedding – that's where I come in.

MAZEL. This isn't just because of me. He deserves it.

SHLIMAZEL. If I didn't know better, I'd say you were getting attached to this kid.

MAZEL. *(Caught, she bristles.)* Don't be ridiculous!

SHLIMAZEL. Look out. When he takes that fall, you're gonna get hurt.

(Lights shift. The **PRINCESS** *clutches her calf.)*

PRINCESS. Ow!

TAM. Princess! What's the matter?

PRINCESS. I seem to have a charley horse in my leg. It's nothing. A trifle.

(She massages her calf with one hand, keeping her head tipped back and pressing the handkerchief to her nose with the other.)

TAM. Can I get you anything? A cold pack? A hot pack?

PRINCESS. Please don't trouble yourself. What were we talking about...?

TAM. I was saying that the instant you entered my life, I became a new man. I discovered I could do things I never... Oh! Princess! Your throat is flushing the color of burning coals...

PRINCESS. Just an allergic reaction...probably a bad shrimp...

TAM. No! I'll get help. *(He calls off left.)* Is there a doctor…

*(**GRILLIDA** tumbles from the shrubbery, where she's been eavesdropping. She quickly smoothes out her dress. **TAM** turns and sees her.)*

Oh, Lady Grillida! Please wait with the Princess while I summon a physician!

*(**TAM** hurries off.)*

GRILLIDA. My lady! I've never seen you in such a state! What ails you?

PRINCESS. Everything at once! My nose is bleeding, there's a cramp in my leg, flushes of heat at my throat…Oh, Grillida! Could this be love? At last?

GRILLIDA. Of course! Just like in your books! You see? The horseshoe. The four leaf clover. The rabbit's foot. All my charms have worked their magic!

*(The **PRINCESS** impulsively hugs **GRILLIDA**. Lights shift back to **MAZEL** and **SHLIMAZEL**.)*

MAZEL. Listen to that ridiculous woman taking credit for my work. Hmph! As if a severed rabbit's foot would be attractive to me. It certainly wasn't lucky for the rabbit! A princess raised on that kind of nonsense…I'm not even sure she's good enough for him!

SHLIMAZEL. Wow. You *have* got it bad! Well, see you later. I've got some business three kingdoms over. Some dumb cluck with new shoes is walking home through a cow pasture…

*(He exits, rubbing his hands with anticipation. **MAZEL** remains, sitting pensively. Light shift back to the **PRINCESS** and **GRILLIDA**.)*

GRILLIDA. There, there, my lady. Are you feeling better now?

PRINCESS. I've never felt better in my life! *(suddenly alarmed)* The symptoms seem to be going away…

(She leaps up.)

I must find Tam!

(She rushes out, bumping into the **KING** *as he enters with* **KAMSTAN**. *She giggles and exits.)*

KING. Lady Grillida, what's happened to the Princess?

GRILLIDA. A miracle, Your Highness! The Princess has found her heart's true love right here in the royal palace!

KAMSTAN. Let me guess – that sweaty little social climber from the village, Tam?

GRILLIDA. Why should the Princess be immune? All the ladies of the court are smitten with him!

KING. This is great news!

KAMSTAN. Your Majesty, might I have a word with you in private?

*(***GRILLIDA*** curtsies and exits one way as the* **KING** *and* **KAMSTAN** *exit the other. Lights shift back to* **MAZEL**, *who is left alone with her thoughts.)*

"WHO KNEW?"

MAZEL.

I WAS ABOVE MERE HUMAN FEELING.
THOSE HEARTS AND FLOWERS SEEMED ABSURD.
LOVE – WHAT COULD BE LESS APPEALING?
TOO SENTIMENTAL,
MUCH TOO MESSY.
THEN I MET TAM. AND I CONFESS HE
OPENED A DOOR
JUST A CRACK,
BUT I'VE SLIPPED THROUGH
AND I CAN'T GO BACK.

SO THIS IS THE WAY IT FEELS TO CARE.
WHO KNEW?
FUNNY, IT CAUGHT ME UNAWARE.
WHO KNEW?
I CONFESS I'M QUITE SURPRISED
THIS COULD EVER BE…
THAT A HUMAN LAD COULD TOUCH
SOMETHING REAL IN ME.

SO HERE'S WHAT THE SHOUTING'S ALL ABOUT.
WHO KNEW?
LOOK AT THE STARS ALL COMING OUT
ON CUE.
BALLADS, I THOUGHT, WERE "BLAH, BLAH, BLAH"
JUST *WORDS* A FOOL WOULD SPEW
BUT I NEVER HEARD ALL THIS *MUSIC…*
WHO KNEW?

(Music continues under, to audience.)

MAZEL. *(cont.)* There! There! Listen! Is that music? Am I
crazy? Do you hear it?

WELL, I GUESS THE JOKE'S ON ME –
ON THIS KID I'M STUCK.
ME, WHO NEVER GOT ATTACHED –
NOW I'M "JUST HIS LUCK!"
I'M GONE AS A GIRL COULD EVER BE.
WHO KNEW?
HEY, WHAT'S A DEMI-DEITY TO DO?
I LET A LITTLE SEED TAKE ROOT;
A LOVELY FLOWER GREW.
AND I GUESS I'M PARTIAL TO FLOWERS.
WHO KNEW?

Scene Six – Kamstan's Private Chambers

KAMSTAN. Your Majesty, have I not always counseled you prudently?

KING. Yes, yes…

KAMSTAN. Then, Your Majesty, I ask you to consider this match. This boy has no kingdom. He brings with him no riches, no political advantage. Can you really allow your royal bloodline to be diluted by the son of mere peasants? I mean, what do we really know about this boy?

KING. Well, he's talented, intelligent, kind, brave…practically perfect.

KAMSTAN. Exactly! Too perfect!

"MORE THAN MEETS THE EYE"

THAT LOYAL AIR.
THE SPEED AND GRACE.
THE TOUSELED HAIR.
THAT OPEN FACE…
COULD ANYONE SO KEEN TO CHARM YOU…
HARM YOU?
THOSE WINNING WAYS.
THE YOUTHFUL PLUCK.
THAT STEADY GAZE.
THE KISS OF LUCK.
COULD SUCH A POSTER-BOY FOR VIRTUE…
HURT YOU?
LET ME ALERT YOU…

I SEE THROUGH HIM;
THERE'S MORE TO HIM
THAN YOU MIGHT BELIEVE.
I'VE A FEELING
HE'S CONCEALING
SOMETHING UP HIS SLEEVE.
RIP OFF THE MASK OF THAT FRIENDLY SMILE,
YOU MAY NOT LIKE WHAT YOU SPY:
SOMETHING SQUISHY,
SOMETHING FISHY –
MORE THAN MEETS THE EYE!

KING. I don't think so. He seems...

KAMSTAN.

> I'M SUSPECTING,
> I'M DETECTING
> HIS DECEITFUL PLOT.

KING. No!

KAMSTAN.

> WATCH YOUR DAUGHTER!

KING. What!?

KAMSTAN.

> IT'S HIS AIM TO
> LAY HIS CLAIM TO
> EV'RYTHING YOU'VE GOT!
> UNDER THAT BOYISH EXTERIOR
> HIDES SOMETHING CUNNING AND SLY.
> CAN'T YOU TELL IT?
> I CAN SMELL IT!
> MORE THAN MEETS THE EYE!
>
> HE'S RISEN TO THE TOP SO EASILY,
> SMILING ALL THE WHILE SO CHEESILY
> ANYONE THAT SLICK AND WEASELY
> YOU OUGHT TO AVOID!
> WHAT HE'LL DO IS INDETERMINATE,
> BUT THE APPLE HAS A WORM IN IT –
> JUST THE KIND OF NASTY VERMIN IT
> PAYS TO HAVE DESTROYED.
>
> BUT WE CAN DO IT ARTFULLY!
> PERMIT ME TO SUGGEST:
> TO KEEP HIM FROM THE PRINCESS. WE CAN PUT HIM
> THROUGH A TEST!

KING. A test? What sort of test?

KAMSTAN. Let him demonstrate the measure of his character. Perhaps...

> (**KAMSTAN** *whispers into the* **KING**'s *ear.*)

KING. But that's next to impossible!

KAMSTAN. Exactly! Legend says it can only be opened by the pure of heart. There's our test!

KING. Kamstan, that's brilliant! I'll convene the court at once!

(The **KING** *rushes off.* **KAMSTAN** *watches him go, then throws back his head and laughs.)*

KAMSTAN.
OH, YOUR HIGHNESS,
YOU ARE MINUS
EVEN HALF A CLUE!
(LIKE YOUR DAUGHTER!)
HOW MUCH WISER
YOUR ADVISER
IS THAN SIMPLE YOU.
I'LL CALL THE TUNE AND YOU'LL DANCE MY JIG;
WHAT I AM SELLING, YOU'LL BUY.
I'LL MISLEAD YOU,
THEN SUCCEED YOU ON THE DAY YOU DIE!
THERE'S MORE TO ME –
TO THE TRUE ME,
SO MUCH MORE THAN MEETS THE EYE!

Scene Seven – The Throne Room

(The COURT *is assembled. The* KING *stands on a raised dais. The* PRINCESS *sits on her throne,* GRILLIDA *at her side.* TAM *kneels before them.* MAZEL *perches above.* PERIAPT *and* MERRYTHOUGHT *skulk on the sidelines.)*

KING. And so, young Tam, do you submit yourself as a worthy suitor for my daughter's hand in marriage?

TAM. *(sincerely)* Could any man be worthy of such a blissful contradiction? A waking dream? Heaven on earth?

PRINCESS. *(a pleasurable twinge)* Ow! *(Everyone reacts.)* ...I'm fine. I'm fine.

KING. Be that as it may, since you are not of royal blood, you must perform a task to prove your worthiness. Kamstan?

*(*KAMSTAN *enters carrying an ornate box and sets it on a pedestal.)*

KAMSTAN. Behold, Tam, the Puzzle Box of Diabolos!

(The COURT *ooh's. Music under.)*

A masterpiece of cunningly contrived sliding panels and interlocking inlays. Can it be opened? Over the centuries a thousand men tried – and failed.

*(*KAMSTAN *is playing to the crowd.* TAM *picks up the box. It falls open in his hands.)*

I myself have spent a lifetime trying to fathom its mysteries...

TAM. Excuse me...

KAMSTAN. Un-breakable. Un-cuttable. God knows, I've tried both...

TAM. Excuse me. Your Grace...

KAMSTAN. You will have twenty-one days...Twenty-one days to succeed where a hundred generations have failed...

TAM. Your Grace? It's open. I hardly touched it...

KAMSTAN. What?!

(Music out.)

PRINCESS. There! You see, Father? Tam has passed your test!

KAMSTAN. *(genuinely consumed with curiosity)* Not so fast! The box! What's inside the box?

TAM. It's empty.

(He looks more closely.)

Well, except for a few mouse droppings.

(The **COURT** *dissolves into chatter.* **KAMSTAN** *is disgusted and mortified.)*

KAMSTAN. Silence! Clearly this box is defective. Anyway, that was...Part One of the test. Your Majesty, might I have a word with you?

*(***KAMSTAN** *and the* **KING** *confer hurriedly.)*

Part Two: It is our desire that you present the Princess with an appropriate token of your intentions.

TAM. Anything.

KAMSTAN. You will proceed from the castle gates and journey towards the rising sun until you come to a sword protruding from a stone.

TAM. Yes, Your Grace.

KAMSTAN. Keep going. Then you will come upon a golden fleece nailed to an oak tree.

TAM. *(with mounting fervor)* Yes, Your Grace.

KAMSTAN. Turn left. Travel until you arrive at the nest of the Hundred Flying Serpents. In the belly of one of them you will find the object of your quest: The Pearl of Wisdom...

(a gasp from the **COURT***)*

...set in The Ring of Truth

(another gasp)

...the selfsame ring that has inscribed about its inside The Secret of Happiness.

(a third gasp)

TAM. If this is the task your majesty desires that I perform,
   I will do it gladly.

KAMSTAN. Pack the provisions!

   (PERIAPT *and* MERRYTHOUGHT *exit.*)

KING. You are not afraid?

   (TAM *flips his coin. MUSIC.*)

TAM. I fear nothing for I have nothing to fear.

PRINCESS. Oh Tam. Don't go! I won't let you! It's too risky.

TAM. What would I not risk for you?

   (*They kiss. The* PRINCESS *rushes off, weeping, followed
   by* GRILLIDA. TAM *calls after them.*)

Don't be afraid. Everything will be fine!

KING. Good! Prepare to depart immediately.

   (*Music. The* COURT *breaks into cheers as* TAM *says his
   goodbyes and exits.* MAZEL *starts after him. A pause in
   the music. The* KING *calls after* TAM…)

And may Luck go with you!

   (MAZEL *does a take to the audience and exits. Music
   buttons the scene.*)

Scene Eight – The Princess' Tower Chamber

(The **PRINCESS** *is up on a stool as a* **SEAMSTRESS** *marks the hem on an elaborate gown.* **GRILLIDA** *reads aloud from one of the romances.)*

GRILLIDA. "…And when the pain was too great he slipped from consciousness. She caressed his face – her fingers trembling over the thousand scars he has suffered to reach her…"

PRINCESS. That's enough. Somehow these books no longer interest me.

GRILLIDA. Tam has been gone six weeks now, my lady. We need to occupy you with something.

PRINCESS. Why don't you take this veil downstairs and put on the trim. I'd like some time alone.

GRILLIDA. As you wish, my lady. But I still say it's bad luck to be making a wedding gown before there's a ring on your finger!

PRINCESS. How could I possibly have bad luck – when you've nailed a horseshoe up over my bed, pressed a four leaf clover in my diary – and you make me wear this ridiculous rabbit's foot around my neck? Please go.

*(***GRILLIDA** *and the* **SEAMSTRESS** *bow and exit. MUSIC. The* **PRINCESS** *moves to her window seat, absently brushing the rabbit's foot against her cheek. The tower unit revolves. Now we're seeing her face framed in the window from the outside.)*

Grillida thinks I believe these charms are magic. She doesn't know I keep them only because they came from you…

"HALF A WORLD AWAY"

PRINCESS.
MY WINDOW SHOWS THE HILLS BELOW –
THE SAME OLD REASSURING VIEW.
BUT FAR BEYOND THOSE HILLS, I KNOW

PRINCESS. *(cont.)*

> YOU'RE SEEING THINGS BOTH STRANGE AND NEW.
> AND WHILE YOU'RE QUESTING FAR AND WIDE,
> I'LL KEEP THIS FEELING LOCKED INSIDE…
>
> HALF A WORLD AWAY.
> STILL YOUR FACE IS ALL I SEE.
> HALF A WORLD AWAY.
> AND I KNOW YOU'RE CLOSE TO ME.
> HOLD ON TO THIS YEARNING,
> THAT'S ALL I CAN DO
> I'M HALF A WORLD AWAY
> FROM YOU.

(On the other side of the stage, **TAM** *appears on his journey.)*

TAM.

> EACH UNTAMED REGION I EXPLORE
> GIVES RISE TO SOMETHING WILDER STILL.
> AND FEELINGS NEVER FELT BEFORE
> BEDEVIL ME TO TEST MY WILL.
> APPROCHING THE FORBIDDEN ZONE,
> I'M LONELY, YES – BUT NOT ALONE.
>
> HALF A WORLD AWAY.
> I CAN FEEL YOUR HAND IN MINE.
> HALF A WORLD AWAY
> AND THE STARS CAN'T MATCH YOUR SHINE.
> KEEP A CANDLE BURNING
> TILL MY JOURNEY'S THROUGH.
> I'M HALF A WORLD AWAY
> FROM YOU.

BOTH.

> OUT OF SIGHT, OUT OF MIND –
> THE BOND WE SHARE IS NOT THAT KIND.
> ON ALL THE EARTH THERE IS NO PLACE
> BEYOND THE WARMTH OF YOUR EMBRACE
>
> HALF A WORLD AWAY
> STILL TWO HEARTS CAN BEAT AS ONE.
> HALF A WORLD AWAY

AND WHEN EV'RY DAY IS DONE,
THERE'S A SWEET RETURNING
WE'LL BE DREAMING OF.
WE'RE HALF A WORLD AWAY.
HALF A WORLD AWAY.
WE'RE ONLY HALF A WORLD AWAY
FROM LOVE.

Scene Nine – Tam's Quest

*(A dance sequence. **TAM** continues to travel. A flying serpent appears. Then another. And another. Soon the stage is swirling with them. **TAM** is hopelessly outnumbered. Suddenly, **MAZEL** is at his side. With **MAZEL**'s help **TAM** slays the flying serpents and recovers the Ring of Truth. He holds it aloft in triumph. [TA-DAA!])*

Scene Ten – Limbo

(**SHLIMAZEL** *enters down left and joins in the applause, continuing after the audience has stopped. As* **TAM** *exits with the ring,* **MAZEL** *crosses to* **SHLIMAZEL**. *A neutral drop comes in behind them.*)

SHLIMAZEL. Bravo! Brilliant! I knew you were good. But I've never seen you work with such style. Such depth.

MAZEL. Well, I've never stuck so long with one person before. That's *your* doing.

SHLIMAZEL. I take full credit. And while you've been stuck with him, what a time I've been having in the rest of the world! The floods! The fires! The pestilence…!

MAZEL. Shlimazel! I never gave a thought to what you might be doing behind my back. *(conflicted)* …But I can't run out on Tam in the eleventh hour…

SHLIMAZEL. You really are something. A career, a love-life. I don't know where you get the energy…

MAZEL. How dare you! I have only one interest in this bet – beating you.

SHLIMAZEL. Right. That's why you're blushing. Anyway, at the end of your year, I'll have one thing to undo. You'll have *millions.* You'll never catch up!

MAZEL. *(making a snap decision)* I'll go right away. Just a quick turn around the world – to keep things from getting too out of hand!

SHLIMAZEL. No! The bet was you had to stay with Tam for a year!

MAZEL. I never said it was exclusive! …Anyway, my work here is done. Tam has the ring! He'll present it to the King, prove his worth, marry the princess. You can't touch him until the year's up.

SHLIMAZEL. Well, you've got me there. You're a shrewd opponent, Mazel.

MAZEL. Tam won't even notice I'm gone. And remember – you don't lay a finger on him!

SHLIMAZEL. All right! All right! I know when I'm outfoxed. If you're going, go!

(**MAZEL** *exits.*)

Goodbye, Miss Charm... You think you put one over on me? You don't even know you've just been played like a balalaika! Tam I don't touch. But I made no promises about the King!

(*Laughing, he exits the other way as a musical TAG buttons the sequence.*)

Scene Eleven – A hilltop overlooking the road that leads to the Royal Palace

*(The **PRINCESS** sits on a bench, embroidering distractedly. Her head is bandaged. **GRILLIDA** enters.)*

GRILLIDA. Good, my lady. Busy hands make the time fly. How is the embroidery progressing?

*(The **PRINCESS** displays the work in her embroidery hoop. It's a total mess.)*

I see your thoughts are elsewhere.

PRINCESS. Three months. Three months. Something must have gone wrong. The horseshoe falling on my head was not a good omen.

GRILLIDA. Now, now. We've put it back up good as new. And look what I have for you here! Something special… An amulet!

*(She holds up an amulet hanging from a silver chain. It is curved and pointed like a large, sharp tooth. She places it around the **PRINCESS**' neck.)*

Ninety days I've soaked it in honey and brine. Honey for love, brine for tears of joy. Plus a little paprika for color. It will bring him back safely, you'll see. From this hilltop we'll be the first to catch sight of Tam as he approaches.

(She pulls a spyglass from her satchel, climbs onto the bench and looks into the distance.)

PRINCESS. Grillida, I know you mean well, but…

GRILLIDA. Your Highness, there's someone coming this way on the south road!

PRINCESS. Give me that spyglass!

*(They switch places. The **PRINCESS** squints into the eyepiece.)*

GRILLIDA. You see? You see? I knew that was a good recipe!

PRINCESS. It is Tam! It is! Oh, Grillida – I think this really may be your doing! Thank you! Thank you!

GRILLIDA. How does he look? Beaten and battle-scarred?

PRINCESS. Not a scratch on him!

GRILLIDA. Road-weary?

PRINCESS. No! There's a spring in his step!

GRILLIDA. Maybe he bagged the quest and went to the beach for three months!

PRINCESS. *(getting down)* He'll be here any moment!

GRILLIDA. But my lady, does he have the ring?

PRINCESS. That I cannot see. Quick! How do I look?

GRILLIDA. There's a blush in your cheek and a shine in your eyes. I wager he'll be glad to see you.

*(*TAM *races on.)*

TAM. And that he is!

PRINCESS. Tam!

(They embrace.)

TAM. And look what I've brought you. The Pearl of Wisdom. Set in the Ring of Truth.

PRINCESS. And is the Secret of Happiness inscribed about the inside?

TAM. Something is. But it's been rubbed away. I can't read it.

(The **PRINCESS** *tips the ring into the light.)*

PRINCESS. It's been slipped on and off too many fingers.

TAM. Well, it will never slip off yours.

(He places the ring on her finger. Bells ring.)

PRINCESS. Let's tell my father!

(All three run off as the scene shifts. MUSIC.)

Scene Twelve – The Royal Throne Room

(The bells continue to ring. The room is ominously empty.
TAM, *the* **PRINCESS,** *and* **GRILLIDA** *enter breathlessly.)*

PRINCESS. Father! Father! Tam has come back! He brought
the ring! Where is everyone?

TAM. Hello! Hello!

*(**KAMSTAN** enters.)*

KAMSTAN. Quiet!

PRINCESS. Kamstan! Such a happy day! How soon can the
wedding take place?

KAMSTAN. Don't you hear those bells! We're in a state of
emergency. The King has taken ill.

PRINCESS. But he was fine at breakfast.

KAMSTAN. These things can be quite sudden.

*(The ringing bells subside. The **KING** is carried in on
an elaborate litter, looking sick indeed. The rest of the
COURT follows solemnly. **SHLIMAZEL** skips in behind
and perches on the edge of the bed. The **PRINCESS** rushes
to the **KING**.)*

PRINCESS. Father!

GRILLIDA. Perhaps I can brew up a cure. I've just received a
shipment of dragon dung.

*(**EVERYONE** looks at her.)*

(defensively) It's very fresh.

KAMSTAN. Silence! The King has no use for you and your
crackpot cures! The Royal Physicians have been examining him. They will make a scientific determination.
Gentlemen, have you reached a consensus? Is there a
cure?

*(The **LEARNED MEN** move to him in a tight group. One
of them hands **KAMSTAN** a slip of paper.)*

The prescription is: "The Milk of a Lion." But this
is impossible! No lioness will give her milk up to a
human! What can we do? Time is running out.

TAM. If that's what it will take to save the King's life, I will get it. I promise.

PRINCESS. No! You just returned.

TAM. The King has been so good to me; it's the least I can do.

KAMSTAN. Quick! Fetch a container in which to put the milk!

(**PERIAPT** *dashes off.*)

Tam, your courage knows no bounds. This will serve as Part Three of your test!

KING. Come close, Tam. You have my word. As soon as I am cured, the wedding will take place.

KAMSTAN. But, mark me, Tam: if you return with the milk of any other animal, surely you will deserve to die.

TAM. So be it.

(**TAM** *rises and turns to the* **PRINCESS.** *Impulsively she takes* **GRILLIDA***'s amulet from her neck and places it around* **TAM***'s.*)

PRINCESS. Tam, I believe this amulet brought you back to me today. I pray it will return you safely to me again.

TAM. I feel the power in it. Coming from you, how could it fail? And I will leave you with a token as well: my lucky gold piece...

(*He takes the gold coin from his pocket and presses it into her hand.*)

Keep it close to you heart.

(*She kisses the coin and places it in the bosom of her dress. They kiss as the rest of the* **COURT** *decorously avert their eyes.* **PERIAPT** *returns bearing a cup with a lid.* **KAMSTAN** *pulls him and* **MERRYTHOUGHT** *into a quick huddle downstage. Uninvited and invisible,* **SHLI-MAZEL** *listens in.*)

KAMSTAN. Periapt, Merrythought...This time I want nothing left to chance. Follow Tam at a discreet distance. And make sure he does not return!

MERRYTHOUGHT. As you wish, your stealthiness.

*(***PERIAPT*** hands ***KAMSTAN*** the cup. He and ***MERRY-THOUGHT*** bow and slink off. ***TAM*** and the ***PRINCESS*** break from their kiss. ***KAMSTAN*** walks over to ***TAM***, playing to the crowd.)*

KAMSTAN. Once again, young Tam, your mettle is about to be tested. This time not only your marriage to the Princess hangs in the balance, but also the life of the King, and the future of the entire kingdom. Good luck.

*(He passes ***TAM*** the cup and puts his arm around him.)*

Now let us all walk with Tam to the castle gates. Let us line the battlements and wave a loving send-off, so when he turns back at the crest of the hill, he will see that the hopes and prayers of the entire kingdom go with him!

*(Music. Everyone exits with ***TAM*** and ***KAMSTAN*** leading the way. The ***KING***'s litter is borne out as well. ***GRIL-LIDA*** puts a consoling arm around the ***PRINCESS*** as they go. Only ***SHLIMAZEL*** remains, barely able to contain his glee.)*

SHLIMAZEL. Goodbye, Tam. Now that you don't have your precious Mazel to smooth the way for you, we'll find out what you're really made of!

Scene Thirteen – Tall Grass & Outside the Lion's Cave

(Music. **TAM** *walks through high grasses.)*

TAM. Every step is harder to take than the last! Why this sense of foreboding? So what if I've had an unreasoning terror of cats since I was a child? ...What could go wrong? I've failed at nothing I've undertaken in months. Why should this be any different? And look – I'm protected by the Princess' amulet. Still...

*(***PERIAPT*** and **MERRYTHOUGHT** *peek though the grass behind him.)*

I feel so...alone.

*(***PERIAPT*** and **MERRYTHOUGHT** *look at each other, then duck behind the grass again.* **TAM** *resumes walking.)*

I've got to get a hold of myself!

"ONLY FEAR"

TAM.

LISTEN, WHO'S THE HERO HERE?
THIS IS JUST A SIMPLE THING.
WHAT IS THERE TO FEAR?
YOU TAKE THE CUP, YOU FILL IT UP,
IS THAT TOO MUCH TO ASK?
WHY AM I SO PETRIFIED?
SOMETHING WITH AN ICY TOUCH
CLUTCHES ME INSIDE.
IT'S CHOKING ME, SQUEEZING ME, GRIPPING ME.
DANGER MAY BE DRAWING NEAR.
NOTHING TO BE SCARED ABOUT –
ONLY FEAR,
ONLY FEAR.

(A cave comes into view. Outside it a lion cub rolls in the grass. **TAM** *spots the cub.)*

Oh look! A little baby lion. See? A lion is just a kind of cat. A cat is nothing to be afraid of. Why should I be frightened now? Here kitty, kitty, kitty...

*(**TAM** wills himself to touch the cub. It reacts playfully. Gingerly, **TAM** "makes friends" with it. Lights cross-fade to the **PRINCESS** in her tower room. She paces tensely.)*

PRINCESS.

STOMACH FULL OF BUTTERFLIES –
COULD IT BE THAT SOMETHING'S WRONG?
PANIC ON THE RISE...
MY LOVE, TAKE CARE! I COULDN'T BEAR
THE PAIN OF LOSING YOU.

*(Lights cross-fade to **KAMSTAN** in his chambers.)*

KAMSTAN.

CERTAIN FEARS ARE JUSTIFIED;
LIONS AREN'T GOATS OR COWS –
LIONS HAVE THEIR PRIDE.
THEY'LL TEAR HIM UP, SMASH HIM UP HIM UP, SLASH HIM
    UP!
THUS MY PROBLEMS DISAPPEAR.
SOON THERE'S NOTHING LEFT OF HIM –
ONLY FEAR,
ONLY FEAR.

*(Lights return us to **TAM**.)*

TAM. Ow! Sharp teeth for such a little fellow. He ran into that cave. That must be where the mother is...

*(**TAM** steels himself.)*

ONE ON ONE WITH WHAT I DREAD TO FACE.
IN MY THROAT MY HEART KEEPS POUNDING FASTER.
RUN, IT SAYS, AND FIND A HIDING PLACE!
EV'RY NERVE IS BRACING FOR DISASTER.
NO! THE TIME TO ACT IS HERE!
WILL I BE A SLAVE TO FEAR
OR WILL I BE ITS MASTER?

NOW THE AIR SEEMS RAREFIED.
ALL MY SENSES QUICKENING.
TINGLING INSIDE.
THE WAY TO WIN IT LET IT IN –
I'LL MAKE A FRIEND OF FRIGHT.

MONSTERS HAVE TO BE EMBRACED.
TERROR IS THE VERY THING.
HEROES HAVE TO TASTE.
TO PROVE MYSELF, SAVE THE KING, WIN MY LOVE
NOW I CROSS A NEW FRONTIER.

WHAT IS THERE TO FRIGHTEN ME?
ONLY FEAR
ONLY FEAR.

IT'S ONLY FEAR
ONLY FEAR.
ONLY FEAR
ONLY FEAR.

(Cup in hand, **TAM** *turns and walks slowly upstage and into the darkness of the cave. There is a deafening ROAR. The curtain falls.)*

End of Act One

ACT TWO

Scene One – Limbo & Tall Grass

(In darkness, a few bars of "The Man Can Do No Wrong." Then a ROAR. MAZEL *appears, perhaps at the back of the house.)*

"IT'S ME"

MAZEL.

WHO'S ON A GIDDY WHIRLWIND TOUR?
IT'S ME!
HELPING TO KEEP THE WORLD SECURE—
IT'S ME!
EV'RYTHING SHLIMAZEL TOUCHED
WAS AN AWFUL MESS!
BUT WHO SET IT ALL TO RIGHTS?
WOULD YOU CARE TO GUESS?

AND OH WHAT A THRILL TO CIRCULATE
ONCE MORE!
I'M EVEN MORE BELOVED THAN BEFORE!
I COULDN'T KEEP A COUNT
OF ALL THE MULTITUDES I KISSED.
BUT THERE'S ONE PARTICULAR PERSON...
I'VE MISSED...

Tam! I never meant to be gone so long – but the bet is all sewn up; what could go wrong? Still, I'd better check...

(A frenzy of primitive drums. Lights up on TAM, *running madly through the high grass. The LIONESS pursues him, perilously close. Grillida's amulet hangs around his neck. He clutches the container of milk.* MAZEL *observes for a moment. She makes a magical pass*

and **TAM** *and the Lioness freeze.* **MAZEL** *speaks as she makes her way to the stage.)*

MAZEL. Tam, Tam, Tam… I turn my back for one minute and look what happens*! (She crosses in.)* I smell Shlimazel's hand in this. *(She fingers the amulet.)* And looks at this ridiculous amulet! *(She whispers into* **TAM**'s *ear.)* Has this brought you luck? Perhaps it's been cursed! Tear it off! Tear it off and throw it away!

(She withdraws to one side and makes another magical pass. The chase resumes. **TAM** *pulls off the amulet and throws it over his shoulder. With a roar the Lioness drops from view behind the grass.* **TAM** *dives forward and disappears into the pit. Blackout)*

Scene Two – The Throne Room

*(**SHLIMAZEL** surveys the scene from above, keeping an eye on a large timepiece he holds in one hand. The **KING** reclines on his litter on the raised dais with **KAMSTAN** on one side and the **PRINCESS** and **GRILLIDA** on the other. The **PRINCESS**, in her wedding dress, is radiantly beautiful – a glittering prize. **KAMSTAN** approaches her, speaking in hushed tones.)*

KAMSTAN. The King hangs on to life by a thread, you highness. I fear Tam will arrive too late to save him – or not at all.

PRINCESS. Tam will be here! And this time there will be no delay before we take our vows!

KAMSTAN. If you're unmarried at the time of your father's death, the kingdom passes to the Prime Minister. Marry me now and you'll still be queen...

*(The **PRINCESS** recoils. Suddenly, triumphal music plays, chimes ring out. A red carpet is unrolled from the door to the **KING**'s bedside. **TAM** enters torn and tattered, but holding the jeweled cup aloft. Members of the **COURT** pour into the room, cheering. Rose petals flutter down on **TAM** from above. He advances toward the dais and bows. **KAMSTAN** retreats in consternation. The **PRINCESS** steps forwards and silences the cheers.)*

PRINCESS. Just as I knew he would, Tam has come back. And what he carries in that cup is more than a promise fulfilled, more than the restoration of the King's good health. It's my happiness, our future, and the future of the kingdom. Please, let's all take a moment of silence to express our thanks for his safe and successful return.

*(All assembled bow their heads. **MAZEL** appears next to **SHLIMAZEL**.)*

MAZEL. You've got some explaining to do!

SHLIMAZEL. Fifteen seconds to spare. You sure know how to cut it close. Don't worry, I've kept my mitts off Tam. He took his last little trip all by himself. And I must say it looks like he performed brilliantly – even without your help.

MAZEL. Sometimes just believing you're lucky can get you halfway there.

SHLIMAZEL. Shhh! We're into the final countdown. ... Eight, seven, six...

(SHLIMAZEL continues to count down silently, eyes glued to the timepiece. The moment of silence is over. TAM approaches the KING.)

TAM. Your Majesty, though the beast pursued me nearly to the palace gates, I outran her – and I have brought you...

(He kneels by the litter and extends the cup as the KING sits up. SHLIMAZEL reaches the end of his countdown.)

SHLIMAZEL. ...ONE!!!

(He points towards TAM. A bolt of lightening connects them for a moment, then lights restore.)

TAM. ...the milk of a dog.

(The KING collapses backwards in shock. A gasp of outrage goes up from the crowd. TAM struggles to speak, but finds his tongue won't work)

KAMSTAN. Milk of a *dog* you've brought us!? You will pay for this with your life!

(KAMSTAN signals the PALACE GUARDS who immediately clap TAM in chains. The PRINCESS takes the cup and passes it off to GRILLIDA. The assembled COURT turns its back on TAM.)

SHLIMAZEL. *(kicking his heels in delight)* One second! One second is all it took me to undo all your work! And you've got to admit – it's original! The wrong word at the wrong moment! Who would think a man's fate could turn on such a trivial thing? It's delicious!

MAZEL. So, he said "dog" when he meant "lion." It could happen to anybody! These are reasonable people. How bad could it be?

SHLIMAZEL. Just wait and see!

Scene Three – A Dungeon

(Lights out on **MAZEL** *and* **SHLIMAZEL**. *The throne room has disappeared. With dizzying speed* **TAM** *has been cast into the palace's deepest darkest dungeon. hestands in chains.)*

TAM. A dog? The milk of a dog!? How could my brain say "lion" and my mouth say "dog"? I'd begun to think I couldn't make a mistake, and now this! I must be stupider than I ever imagined!

*(***KAMSTAN** *enters.)*

KAMSTAN. So! My treasonous young friend – at last you show your true colors!

TAM. Kamstan! Please! That milk! It will save the King's life! Have him drink it before it's too late!

KAMSTAN. How wicked you are, Tam. How full of lies. Ironic that at the crucial moment you tripped over your own tongue and told the truth!

TAM. If only you would permit the Princess to see me, I'm sure I could make her understand...

KAMSTAN. Do you imagine the Princess desires to ever lay eyes on you again?

TAM. I'm sure she must be upset, but...

KAMSTAN. Who did you think you were? Did you really believe you could marry a princess? You!? Didn't you think I'd check up on you Tam? I, who leave nothing to chance? "The unlucky son of the unlucky son of an unlucky man." That's what they say about you in the village. But you and I both know there's no such thing as bad luck. Just laziness. Low standards. Poor judgment. That's your birthright, Tam. Not exactly the kind of pedigree a Princess requires in a mate. Isn't that right?

TAM. Yes.

KAMSTAN. Doesn't she deserve someone perfect? Someone wonderful?

TAM. Yes.

KAMSTAN. Oh, you could fool everyone – even yourself – for a little while. But in the end, you are what you are. Blood will tell, Tam. You thought you could "B-Positive." But now you're "O-Negative." It's really rather funny when you think about it.

"THE LUCKIEST MAN ALIVE"

KAMSTAN.

NOW COMES THE PUNCH LINE YOU SHOULD HAVE
    FORSEEN ALL ALONG.
OH, BUT THE FATES ARE FAR CRUELER THAN YOU COULD
    HAVE KNOWN.
SETTING YOU UP FOR A TRULY SPECTACULAR PLUNGE
CAUSED BY A SLIP-UP THAT'S NOBODY'S FAULT BUT YOUR
    OWN!
BANG! AND DOWN YOUR FUTURE CRASHES!
BANG! YOUR PAST HAS OVERCOME YOU!
BANG! YOU LITTLE SCHEME IN ASHES!
BANG! THE PRINCESS TAKEN FROM YOU!

THERE YOU STAND,
A BROKEN MAN.
LOWER THAN
WHEN YOU BEGAN…

Clapped into chains. Hanged at dawn. You'd have been better off if you'd never left that filthy pile of rubble you called home!

TAM. *(quietly)* Oh no, Kamstan. You're wrong.

I'VE KNOWN LOVE
I'VE FLOWN HIGH
I'VE
SHOWN MYSELF I'M NOT FRIGHTENED TO DIE
HERE I STAND,
THE LUCKIEST MAN ALIVE.

KAMSTAN. You're terrified. Why don't you admit it?

TAM.

I'VE HAD JOY
UNSURPASSED
I'VE
SHARED A KISS FAR TOO
    PERFECT TO LAST
HERE I STAND
THE LUCKIEST MAN ALIVE.

KAMSTAN.

SOON THE NOOSE
PUTS AN END TO ALL YOUR
LYING
AT LAST THIS FARCE
IS THROUGH. LOOK AT YOU...
THE LUCKIEST MAN ALIVE.

KAMSTAN. And where has all that luck brought you?

TAM.

IF I LIVED A DREAM
I'M PREPARED TO WAKE
    FROM IT
EVEN THOUGH THE DREAM
    WAS BRIEF
I'M GLAD FOR WHAT I TAKE
    FROM IT:

KAMSTAN.

WAKE UP AND
SEE... THE NIGHTMARE
    YOU'VE
WROUGHT ALL.
FOR NAUGHT...FOR
    NOTHING AT ALL.

TAM. To know the Princess? Who could put a price on that?

TAM.

ONE WHOLE YEAR
I HAD HER.
I WOULDN'T TRADE THAT
FOR ALL THE LIFETIMES
    THAT WILL BE OR WERE
SO I BOW
TO WHAT'S IN STORE
I FILLED MY PLATE FULL OF
    LIFE, HOW UNGRATEFUL
    I'D BE TO WANT MORE
I'LL THANK HEAVEN FOR
    HER
WITH MY VERY LAST BREATH.
THOSE FEW MOMENTS WE
    SHARED
LET ME GO TO MY DEATH
THE LUCKIEST MAN
THE LUCKIEST MAN ALIVE!

KAMSTAN.

ALL YOUR TEARS
ALL YOUR WHIMPERING FOR
MER-
CY...WON'T SAVE YOU NOW!
TO THE GALLOWS
COMES THE DAWN YOU'LL BE
GONE...
WHILE I SUR – VIVE!
DOWN...
YOU...GO...
IT'S OVER...
FOR THE LUCKIEST MAN...
THE LUCKIEST MAN ALIVE

Scene Four – The Princess' Tower Room

(The Princess' chambers. **PRINCESS** *has flung herself across her bed where she weeps uncontrollably.* **GRILLIDA** *paces, wringing her hands.)*

GRILLIDA. My lady, please. Don't thrash about so. You'll ruin the veil.

PRINCESS. What good is a wedding dress when there can be no wedding? What a fool I've been – mistaking every itch, every twinge, every pimple for love! Now I know what those books were talking about! I have discovered the true depth of my love only in losing Tam!

GRILLIDA. Can you not plead Tam's case to the King?

PRINCESS. Kamstan says the King is too angry to see me! We're Tam's only hope. There must be something in that sack of yours! A hack-saw?

GRILLIDA. No, my lady. But don't despair! I think it's time to consult my recipe book. *(She pulls a small notebook from her bosom and leafs through it.)* Let's see…tonics, physics, philters. A potion for every occasion.

PRINCESS. Grillida! Where did you get that book?

GRILLIDA. I bought it many years ago from a traveling snake-oil salesman.

PRINCESS. What's the title?

GRILLIDA. *(Showing her the cover.)* "Cooking with Snake-Oil." Perhaps we can find something to bring about a change of heart in the King…

PRINCESS. That's no good! He won't receive us.

GRILLIDA. Something to render Tam's neck impervious to the noose?

PRINCESS. Tam is beyond our reach, under lock and key.

GRILLIDA. Something to make the Hangman bungle his job?

PRINCESS. *(A ray of hope.)* Maybe.

GRILLIDA. All right. Here we are! What do we need? Snake-oil – naturally… A dollop of quicksand. Check. The sweat of an honest man…I think we're going to be fine.

PRINCESS. You have those things?

"WASTE NOT, WANT NOT" REPRISE

GRILLIDA. Of course…

WASTE NOT, WANT NOT
COUNT ON ME
LET'S REVIEW THE RECIPE:
SOME WOOL OF BAT –
THAT WE'VE GOT.
MUMMY DUST. Check.
CAMEL SNOT. Yup.

WASTE NOT, WANT NOT
THAT IS WHY
WHAT WE NEED I CAN SUPPLY!
YOU KNOW HOW CRAZY TO
SAVE I AM
AND NOW WE'RE
SAVING TAM…

(MUSIC continues under.)

Let's see, what else…? A hair from the head of a virgin…

(She regards the **PRINCESS** *dubiously. A beat. Primly the* **PRINCESS** *plucks a hair and hands it over.)*

PRINCESS. Not that it's any of your business.

GRILLIDA. *(back to the list)* A pterodactyl's tongue…

PRINCESS. How old *is* that book!?

GRILLIDA. It's been out of print for years…. Oh no! The jar is empty! I'm fresh out of pterodactyl tongues! And pterodactyls are extinct!

PRINCESS. Maybe you could substitute something.

GRILLIDA. No! The instructions are clear. The formulas must be followed to the letter or they're not magic – they're just disgusting.

PRINCESS. Every avenue is barred to us! Poor Tam!

> *(The* **PRINCESS** *throws herself into* **GRILLIDA***'s arms and weeps inconsolably.)*

GRILLIDA. This has never happened before!
IT'S AS IF SOME COSMIC JOKER
PLAYED A TRICK THAT GUARANTEED
I'D HAVE EVERYTHING ON HAND –
ALL EXCEPT THE THING I NEED!

> *(MUSIC continues under.)*

There, there, my Lady. We did our best . Go ahead and cry.

THE DOOM THE FATES DECREE CAN'T BE ERASED
IT'S A TERRIBLE CURSE – AND WHAT'S EVEN WORSE,
IT'S AN AWFUL WASTE!

Scene Five – A Forgotten Wine Cellar Deep Beneath the Palace

(Vaulted arches. Rows of casks, barrels, racks of bottles recede into the shadows. Everything is covered with cobwebs. **SHLIMAZEL** *perches on a large barrel at center.)*

SHLIMAZEL. All your work destroyed in one second! Who's more powerful? Go on – say it!

MAZEL. Shlimazel, you've won. Congratulations.

SHLIMAZEL. The milk of... a dog! *(laughing)* Wham! He never knew what hit him! Did you see his face?

MAZEL. I'll never forget it.

SHLIMAZEL. Speaking of which... *(looking around)* You've brought me all the way down here. The Wine of Forgetfulness? Where is it?

MAZEL. You're sitting on it.

SHLIMAZEL. What?!?!

*(***SHLIMAZEL*** jumps off the barrel.* **MAZEL** *produces a goblet and fills it from a spigot on the barrel's side)*

Wow! You didn't skimp. You're a class act, Mazel.

MAZEL. *(Handing him the goblet.)* Here. Drink up.

*(***SHLIMAZEL*** drinks the wine in one gulp.* **MAZEL** *refills the goblet.)*

It's not easy to come by, you know. I had to call in a lot of favors.

SHLIMAZEL. Come on – you have a drink too!

MAZEL. No, Shlimazel. Forgetfulness is not for me.

SHLIMAZEL. Your problem is you don't know a good thing when it's right under your nose. Oh well – (*He looks blankly at* **MAZEL**.*)* What were we talking about?

MAZEL. The Wine of Forgetfulness. There. In the glass you're holding.

SHLIMAZEL. Wow! This is a good batch! *(He drinks again.)* I always find there's nothing like a few glasses of wine to raise the spirits.

(A trap door opens and a grotesque **IMP** *pops up through the floor.)*

SHLIMAZEL. *(cont.)* Look!

(Another **IMP** *rises through another trap door.)*

Here they come now! Spirits! Goblins! Gremlins! Tricksters!

(One rears back and hisses at **MAZEL.***)*

MAZEL. Charming friends you have, Shlimazel.

SHLIMAZEL. You're scaring them. Do you mind? If you're not going to drink, maybe you'd better take off.

MAZEL. With pleasure. *(She starts to go, then turns.)* But Shlimazel. The debt is now paid. We're even.

SHLIMAZEL. Just remember – Tam is still mine for a year. You can't save him.

MAZEL. As you say, Shlimazel. I'll keep my part of the bargain.

(She vanishes.)

SHLIMAZEL. Aw, go on, Miss. Good-sportsmanship! I don't need any kill-joys around on a night like this!

(He turns to his hellish **DRINKING COMPANIONS** *and brags.)*

"SHLIMAZEL'S WALTZ"

SCHLIMAZEL.

MAZEL AND I HAD A WAGER
WE PUT OUR TRICKS TO THE TEST
OH YES, THE QUESTION WAS MAJOR:
WHICH OF THE BETTORS WAS BEST?
NOW ON THIS FESTIVE OCCASION,
IT'S ONLY FITTING THAT YOU –
FRIENDS OF THE FIENDISH PERSUASION –
GIVE OLD SHLIMAZEL HIS DUE.

HERE'S TO ME!
THOUGH I KNOW IT'S UNSEEMLY TO BOAST
COME AND JOIN IN A VICTORY TOAST!
WE'LL DRINK TILL THE BARREL IS DRY!

SCHLIMAZEL. *(cont.)*

> DRINK TO ME!
> NOW SHLIMAZEL GOES RIGHT TO THE TOP!
> NOW THE ACCOLADES NEVER WILL STOP!
> FOR SUCH AN UNPOPULAR GUY,
> I COULDN'T CLIMB ANY HIGHER!
>
> TRIUMPH! WHAT A TRIUMPH!
> I'LL BE LIONIZED IN
> PERPETUITY!
> GENIUS! WHAT A GENIUS!
> I'M THE MONARCH OF THE DARKER SIDE.
>
> HOW DID I DO IT?
> IT WASN'T EASY.
> I WAS A FOUL-UP FROM THE TIME I WAS A LAD –
> A LITTLE HOODLUM ONLY GOOD AT BEING BAD.
> FROM A PARIAH WHO WAS CAST ASIDE
> AND SPAT UPON AND SHAT UPON AND SCORNED.
>
> HOW DID I RISE TO RULE THIS MISBEGOTTEN HORDE –
> THE SCALED, THE WINGED, THE CLOVEN HOOFED, THE
>   HORNED?
> FROM STANDARD ISSUE IMP IN THE DEMONIC RANK AND
>   FILE
> HOW DID I GET TO THE TOP OF THE PILE?
> HOW DID I TURN OUT SO CRAFTLY, CUNNINGLY,
> TOTALLY STUNNINGLY VILE?
>
> Well, it took a lot of hard work, I'll tell you – but you
> know, I always say…

ALL. *(interrupting him)*

> HERE'S TO YOU!
> RAISE A GLASS TO YOUR TALENT AND SPUNK!
> CHEERING SPIRITS ARE MEANT TO BE DRUNK –
> THIS WINE MAKES OUR CRANIUMS HUM.
>
> DRINK TO YOU!
> NOW YOU'LL FINALLY GET SOME RESPECT!

SHLIMAZEL.

> THOUGH FOR WHAT I CANNOT RECOLLECT…
> I'M FEELING EFFECTIVELY NUMB.

ALL.

COME! LIFT A TUMBLER TO SOMEONE...

FAMOUS! NOW YOU'RE FAMOUS!
THOUGH YOU NAME HAS SOMEHOW
SLIPPED OUR MEMORY.
GENIUS! WHAT A GENIUS!
YOU'RE THE MONARCH OF THE DARKER SIDE

SHLIMAZEL. Let's have another!

HERE'S TO AMNESIA. THAT SWEET ANASTHESIA
THAT EASES THE PAIN OF THE PAST.

ALL.

HERE'S TO THE BLURRING ALREADY OCCURING
AS WE GET COLLECTIVLY PLAST-ERED!

LA LA! LA LA LA LA!
WE FORGET THE WORDS, BUT
FILL THE GLASS AGAIN!
LA LA! LA LA LA LA!
WE'RE HAPPY BEYOND ANY DOUBT!

SHLIMAZEL.

BUT WHAT ARE WE SINGING ABOUT...?

ALL.

LA LA LA LA LA LA LA LA —AH!

SHLIMAZEL.

MONARCH OF THE DARKER SIDE!

ALL.

(LA-LA-LA, LA-LA-LA, LA-LA-LA, LA-LA-LA-LA!) HEY!

Scene Six – Kamstan's Chambers

(**KAMSTAN** *is bawling out* **PERIAPT** *and* **MERRY-THOUGHT**)

KAMSTAN. You idiots!!!! I thought you were going to see to it that Tam never made it back here! What happened?

PERIAPT. We figured if a lion was going to tear him limb from limb, why should we have blood on our hands?

KAMSTAN. But he never found a lion...

MERRYTHOUGHT. Yes, he did! And he got the milk, too!

PERIAPT. He must have put that lion into a trance of something...

MERRYTHOUGHT. But then as he left she came tearing out of that cave after him! They ran so fast we couldn't keep up! We figured she'd catch him eventually...

PERIAPT. Or at least he'd spill the milk...

KAMSTAN. He said it was the milk of a dog! He must have lost his mind with fright. And what became of the lion?

MERRYTHOUGHT. It's roving about the countryside! As we approached the village we could hear it roaring! The townspeople are terrified. They've barricaded themselves in their houses!

KAMSTAN. This is not good. Not good at all. A female lion in the vicinity will raise questions that might postpone the execution. Not to mention that it is the source of the one thing that could save the King's life! No! I haven't gotten this close to the throne to be pushed off now! There's only one thing to do!

MERRYTHOUGHT & PERIAPT. What, your Excellency?

KAMSTAN. The two of you have got to kill that lion before the sun comes up!

Scene Seven – The Princess' Tower Room

(**PRINCESS** *sits in her window.* **GRILLIDA** *snores softly in a chair.*)

"GOODBYE"

PRINCESS.

> THE NIGHT'S ALIVE WITH DREAD.
> IT PRICKLES ON MY ARMS.
> THE AIR IS FAIRLY SHIVERING
> WITH WARNINGS AND ALARMS.
>
> THE MOON IS FAR TOO BRIGHT.
> IT LIGHTS A WORLD GONE MAD
> WHERE EV'RY HOPE IS BLOWN APART
> AND GOOD GIVES WAY TO BAD.

Good fortune smiled on us once. Could it not make a last minute return? Heads!

(She takes **TAM***'s coin from her bosom and flips it one last time. It falls to the floor and rolls down a grate with an ominous resounding clink. Disconsolate, she goes to the window.)*

> NOW DEATH BEGINS TO BECKON ME
> FROM DEEP WITHIN THE MOAT.
> I'LL THROW THE WINDOW WIDE AND JUMP...

(She opens the window, climbs onto the sill, and hesitates...)

> BUT FIRST I'LL WRITE A NOTE.

(She retreats to her writing desk, takes up a pen and paper, thinks for a moment, and starts to compose.)

Dear Grillida,

> GOODBYE! GOODBYE!
> DO NOT WEEP OR GRIEVE.
> DON'T HEAVE A SIGH,
> IT'S TIME FOR ME TO LEAVE.
> IT'S LATE, TOO LATE!
> EXCUSE ME WHILE I FLY.

PRINCESS. *(cont.)*

I BOW TO FATE.
I HATE A DATE
AT HEAVEN'S GATE –
GOODBYE!

(A ROAR from the fields outside the window draws her attention.)

NOW, WHAT WAS THAT? I COULD HAVE SWORN
I HEARD A SORT OF ROARING.
UNLESS, OF COURSE, IT'S GRILLIDA –
SHE'S AWF'LY PRONE TO SNORING.

NO! I THINK IT'S MORE THAN THAT.
IT MIGHT BE WORTH EXPLORING.
COULD IT BE?
LET ME SEE...

THE SCENE'S AGLOW BENEATH THE LUNAR GLARE.
BUT NOT A LIVING CREATURE MOVES ABOUT.
THE SILENCE IS TOO MUCH FOR ME TO BEAR,
FOR NOW IT'S MY OWN SANITY I DOUBT.
AM I HALUCINATING,
FABRICATING,
SOUNDS THAT ARE NOT THERE?

Where was I?

(She returns to the letter.)

GOODBYE! GOODBYE!
TO MY DOOM I GO.
I'LL MEET MY LOVE
ABOVE, LOOK OUT BELOW!
TO DEATH I DASH.
MY FINAL CURTAIN'S NIGH.
THROW WIDE THE SASH!
IT MAY BE RASH,
BUT DOWN I SPLASH...

(Another ROAR. She lays down her pen and rushes to the window.)

PRINCESS. *(cont.)*

> OF COURSE THAT WAS A ROAR,
> BUT CAN I CREDIT WHAT I'M SEEING?
> PERIAPT AND MERRYTHOUGHT. ACROSS THE FIELD ARE
>   FLEEING!
>
> FOLLOWED BY A LIONESS!
> AHA! PERHAPS I'M BEING
> TOO "TRAGIQUE"
> FRAIL AND WEAK.
>
> I'VE NEVER BEEN OF THE HEROIC ILK.
> I ALWAYS TURN TO JELLY IN A JAM.
> BUT IF I GET THAT LIONESS' MILK.
> A HERO MIGHT BE JUST THE THING I AM!
> IF I CAN CURE THE KING. THEN MIGHT HE NOT
> RELENT AND PARDON TAM!?

(A third ROAR galvanizes her into action.)

It's a desperate chance, but what do we have to lose? How a beast like that came to wander past my window I can't stop to question. I have to take action now! Be strong, Tam – help is on the way!

> ...IT'S UP TO ME –
> AT LEAST I'VE GOT TO TRY!
> I CAN'T DELAY!
> I'LL SEIZE THE DAY!
> I'M OFF! AWAY!
> GOODBYE!

(She grabs her cloak and rushes out the door. **GRILLIDA**, *a heavy sleeper, continues to doze in the chair as the lights fade. A special lingers on the unfinished note – forgotten on the* **PRINCESS**' *writing table.)*

Scene Eight – The Palace Courtyard

*(Pre-dawn. A stark gallows stands at center. Offstage
DRUMMERS mark a steady, muffled beat. The court
has gathered. The* **KING**, *looking like death itself, has
been carried out on his litter.* **KAMSTAN**, *surrounded by
his coterie of* **FLATTERERS**, *tries to conceal his eagerness.*
GRILLIDA *sobs into a handkerchief.* **TAM** *is marched
out under heavy guard and ascends to the gallows. The*
HANGSMAN *places the noose around* **TAM**'s *neck.* **TAM**
*closes his eyes, as though praying... There's a magi-
cal sound and a dramatic lighting change. All action
freezes.* **MAZEL** *appears on the gallows. She whispers into*
TAM's *ear.)*

MAZEL. Tam! Tam! I can't help you now. You have to help
yourself! Please! I see you've resigned yourself to this
fate. You are meant for better things, Tam. Even now
happiness is within your reach... I've never shown
myself to a mortal before, but you're a special case.
See me, Tam. Open your eyes.

*(***TAM**'s *eyes open. Music under.)*

TAM. Who are you?

MAZEL. My name is Mazel. It was I who brought you luck.

TAM. And are you here to save me from this?

MAZEL. No. I cannot save you.

TAM. So you've abandoned me when I need you the most?
I don't care for myself, but you have broken the Princess' heart. How cruel you are! How selfish!

MAZEL. Selfish I am. And vain. And shallow. But I've
learned to care for you, Tam. And I'm prepared to tell
you something that I've never told another soul. It's a
secret. If it ever became common knowledge it could
make me obsolete.

TAM. Are you saying there's another way to acquire luck?

MAZEL. Yes, a better way.

"INSIDE"

MAZEL.

> TAM, I FAILED YOU.
> NOW I CAN'T LET YOU OFF THE HOOK.
> BUT LUCK IS WITHIN YOUR REACH –
> IF YOU KNOW WHERE TO LOOK...
>
> INSIDE
> YOU HAVE ALL YOU NEED
> TO REALIZE YOUR DREAMS.
>
> INSIDE
> YOU CAN CHANGE YOUR FATE.
> CRAZY AS IT SEEMS.
>
> THAT'S THE SECRET
> VERY FEW HAVE KNOWN.
> YOU DON'T HAVE TO PRAY FOR LUCK,
> YOU CAN MAKE YOUR OWN.
>
> INSIDE
> YOU POSSESS THE MEANS
> TO STARTLE AND ASTOUND.
> INSIDE!
> THERE'S A POWER THERE
> WAITING TO BE FOUND.
>
> YOU'LL DISCOVER
> WHEN YOUR HOPES GROW THIN
> ME YOU CAN GET BY WITHOUT,
> IF YOU LOOK WITHIN...

TAM. But I wouldn't know how to start. Everything good that's happened to me was your doing.

MAZEL. That's not true. You have a good and kind heart. You'd be surprised how much easier that's made my job.

TAM. I don't know...

MAZEL. You've already done it. I wasn't with you in the lion's cave. You thought I was protecting you, but I wasn't. You did that all by yourself.

TAM. What should I do?

MAZEL. That's up to you now. Be bold. Take a leap of faith. Whatever pops up in your path, you can handle it.

MAZEL/TAM.

SO
INSIDE
ALL YOUR/MY TOMORROWS BEGIN
INSIDE
YOU/I HAVE A BATTLE TO WIN!

TAM.

I CARRY IN ME

MAZEL.

NOT GIVING UP,

TAM.

ALL OF THE LUCK

MAZEL.

NOT TURNING BACK

TAM.

I EVER DREAMED OF

MAZEL.

YOU'LL MAKE THE LUCK
OTHERS MAY LACK.
IN YOUR DARKEST MOMENT,
YOU CAN TURN THE TIDE.

TAM.

I'VE GOT TO...

MAZEL/TAM.

TRUST IN THE LUCK...
TRUST IN THE LUCK...

TRUST IN THE LUCK YOU/I MAKE
INSIDE.

TAM. How can I thank you?

MAZEL. Be happy. You won't remember that we had this little talk. But you will remember what we talked about.

(She clasps his hand and kisses him on the cheek.)

Now, close your eyes...

(He does. She smoothes his hair then steps away. Lights restore. The drum roll resumes. The **HANGSMAN** *tightens the noose around* **TAM** *'s neck and moves to the lever which will spring the trap door under* **TAM** *'s feet.* **TAM** *appears to be processing an idea. Suddenly...)*

TAM. WAIT!!!

(The drumming ceases. There is a gasp from the crowd. **TAM** *is improvising, but he seems in control and confident.)*

My lords, it is the custom, before the condemned dies, to give him one last wish. My wish is to speak with the King.

KAMSTAN. Is there no end to this fellow's tricks? The King is gravely ill. He has not the time or energy to hear what you have to say!

TAM. I believe that while the King still breathes the decision is his, not yours. Your Majesty, what say you?

(All eyes go to the **KING.** *)*

KING. The boy has a point, Kamstan. I'm not dead yet. Speak, Tam.

TAM. Your Majesty, it is known that the lion is the king of animals. Yet in comparison with you, My Lord, a lion is no more than a dog. I called the lioness a dog as an expression of my respect and admiration for Your Majesty. I beg you, drink her milk, and it will make you well. I swear on my love for the Princess that I am telling the truth.

KAMSTAN. How unfortunate we cannot put your little fabrication to the test. The milk has been poured out.

GRILLIDA. WAIT!!!

(All eyes go to **GRILLIDA** *who pulls the milk container from her satchel.)*

I saved it.

KAMSTAN. Surely that milk has curdled by now.

*(***GRILLIDA** *removes the lid and takes a sniff.)*

GRILLIDA. No, it's fresh.

> (**SHLIMAZEL** *bangs up through a trap door at center stage. Of course, he is invisible to all present. He rests his elbow on the stage floor, clutching his head.*)

TAM. Grillida! Hurry! Let the King put that cup to his lips at once.

> (**GRILLIDA** *rushes towards the* **KING** *and trips over* **SCHLIMAZEL.** *The milk spills. The* **CROWD** *gasps.*)

Lady, Grillida! How could this happen?

GRILLIDA. I stumbled.

TAM. Over what?

GRILLIDA. I don't know!

> (*She wails.*)

SHLIMAZEL. (*flinching*) Oooh, what a hangover.

KAMSTAN. (*thrusting a handkerchief at* **GRILLIDA**) There, there. No use crying over...well... (*He gestures to the white puddle on the floor.*)

TAM. Your Highness, I don't know what to say...

KING. It's not your fault, Tam. This was a trick of fate. Nonetheless, today you shall have my daughter's hand in marriage. Come down from the scaffold, Tam! Lady Grillida! Stop your weeping and go fetch the Princess.

GRILLIDA. (*crying even more loudly*) Oh, was there ever a day so black? I thought you both were as good as dead! I sought to protect you from this news, but now I see I cannot!

> (**TAM** *rushes down from the scaffold. She takes the Princess' note from her bodice and hands it to him.*)

The Princess lies at the bottom of the moat. I found this letter in her chamber just before daybreak.

TAM. No! Oh, Your Highness, if only I could be in your place – for you will surely see the Princess again before I do...

PRINCESS' VOICE. WAIT!!!

(The **PRINCESS** *enters leading the LIONESS. The* **CROWD** *gasps and draws back.)*

PRINCESS. Tam, now no one can doubt that you're providing the milk of a lion.

TAM. But how? How did this happen?

PRINCESS. I saw her from my window last night chasing Periapt and Merrythought. I realized that here was the means to revive the King, so I set off in pursuit. By the time I caught up with her she seemed much less ferocious.

TAM. What brought about the change?

PRINCESS. I believe she had just eaten a very large meal.

*(***KAMSTAN** *reacts to this.)*

As I drew close I could see she had something in her paw, which was giving her pain. She let me pull it out. And here it is.

(She holds up the amulet.)

TAM. Grillida's amulet!

GRILLIDA. You see? I told you it would bring you luck!

PRINCESS. Ever since then she has followed me like a devoted pet.

KAMSTAN. *(stepping forward unctuously)* Your Majesty, we all rejoice at this extraordinary turn of events...

(The LIONESS growls and he jumps back.)

PRINCESS. I don't believe she wants other people near her. But if I stroke her head perhaps she will let Tam take a little milk – since he's done it once before.

(As **PRINCESS** *rubs the LIONESS' ears,* **TAM** *advances cautiously with the cup. The* **ONLOOKERS** *gather around, screening the actual milking from the audience.* **MAZEL** *appears and helps* **SHLIMAZEL** *up onto the stage, closing the trap with a bang.)*

SHLIMAZEL. Ow! Please, my head!

MAZEL. Well, it looks like you tied one on last night. What was the occasion?

SHLIMAZEL. I forget. What's going on here anyway? Who are these people? How did we get here?

MAZEL. *(an aside)* That really *was* a good batch.

*(She walks **SHLIMAZEL** over to **KAMSTAN** who stands alone to one side of the stage.)*

Shlimazel, there's someone here I think you should meet. He leaves nothing to chance. He doesn't even believe in luck.

SHLIMAZEL. Oh no? Well, he's going to believe in *me*! Come on, pal. I think this is the beginning of a beautiful friendship.

*(**SHLIMAZEL** slings an arm around **KAMSTAN**'s neck, and they exit together.)*

*(MUSIC. The **CROWD** parts. **TAM** carries the cup to the **KING**, who drinks the contents. The **KING** rises, unsteadily at first.)*

PRINCESS. Father! The color has returned to your cheeks!

KING. I... I... I've never felt better. It's quite miraculous! And you've both had a hand in effecting this cure. You've kept your part of the bargain, so let me keep mine. The wedding shall take place immediately. *(The **COURT** cheers.)* Witness, all you present, the union of the Princess and Tam in marriage – a pair matched in beauty and bravery. A couple who will one day rule this kingdom with wisdom and courage. Tam, do you take my daughter to love, honor, and protect, till death do you part?

TAM. I do.

KING. My child, do you take Tam to love, honor, and protect till death do you part?

PRINCESS. I do.

KING. Tam, take the ring from her right hand.

*(**TAM** slips the ring from the **PRINCESS**' right hand. **MAZEL** steps in and freezes the action. Magic SFX.)*

MAZEL. See me, Tam. Remember me.

TAM. You! I should have known. I can never thank you enough!

MAZEL. I wish I could the credit, but I can't. You and the Princess saved the day with your own quick thinking and bold actions. It's I who should be thanking you.

TAM. Me? But why?

MAZEL. You put a face on humanity for me, Tam. And such a sweet face. You've helped me reach an important decision. What's written inside that ring is a secret I never wanted the world to know. But now I see how selfish I was. People will be happier knowing they control their own fates. Read the inscription to the crowd, Tam. Give everyone the benefit of its message.

TAM. But the inscription has been rubbed away.

(**MAZEL** *takes the ring, blows through it – magic SFX. She returns it to him.*)

MAZEL. You'll be able to read it now. Go now. With my blessing. Goodbye, Tam. I'll never forget you.

(**MAZEL** *unfreezes the action.* **TAM** *addresses the crowd. Unobserved,* **SHLIMAZEL** *enters.*)

TAM. As our gift to all those gathered here today, the Princess and I would like to share with you the Secret of Happiness…inscribed about the Ring of Truth…set with the Pearl of Wisdom.

(*There is a collective, "Oooh," from the* **CROWD**. **TAM** *tips the ring to the light and reads.*)

"The Secret of Happiness is to be Lucky. And the Secret of Luck is to Make Your Own."

(*A collective "Ahhh," of understanding.*)

KING. Now then, Tam. Place the ring on the fourth finger of the Princess' left hand.

(**TAM** *does.*)

I pronounce you man and wife.

(**TAM** *and the* **PRINCESS** *kiss. The* **CROWD** *cheers, closing around them to wish them well.* **MAZEL** *stands on the periphery, dabbing a tear from her eye.* **SHLIMAZEL** *joins her.*)

SHLIMAZEL. So! What do you say we move on?

MAZEL. Shlimazel! You're back.

SHLIMAZEL. I always come back. That broken down loser you hooked me up with is a bore. You know what I say? Immortality is too short to spend with a creep like that. Besides, I belong with you.

MAZEL. Too late. I'm out of business.

SHLIMAZEL. What!?

MAZEL. Yes. Now everyone has heard the inscription in the ring. The word will spread. It's done. I'm obsolete. I'll retire. Plant a little garden. Catch up on my reading. It won't be so bad...

SHLIMAZEL. What are you, crazy? After all these years haven't you learned a thing about human nature? Ten minutes from now that bunch won't even remember your inscription! People are lazy! They don't want to make their own luck. They want to believe in *us*! Good Luck and Bad Luck! Hap and Mishap! You and me. We'll never be obsolete! Why, we're just getting started! We're gonna diversify. Lotteries. Scratch 'n Win cards. Whole cities dedicated to gambling! Everybody's gonna want you – but mostly they'll get me. It's a beautiful system. Why mess with it?

MAZEL. Maybe you're right.

SHLIMAZEL. Of course I'm right! Look at them! All wishing the happy couple good luck! They don't get it, and they never will!

"LUCK!" FINALE

SHLIMAZEL.
> WE'RE A
> DOUBLE ACT THAT
> NOTHIN'S GONNA SEVER...
> KID, WE'RE GOIN' ON FOREVER...

MAZEL, SHLIMAZEL & CHORUS.	TAM & PRINCESS.
NOTHING'LL MAKE A MAN IMMUNE TO LUCK.	INSIDE…
LUCK IS A FACTOR THAT YOU CANNOT PLAN.	ALL OUR TOMORROWS ARE INSIDE…
LUCK IS A THING TO FLUCTUATE; LUCK DISAPPEARS, AND THEN LUCK IN A FLASH'LL CHANGE YOUR FATE – THEN CHANGE IT BACK AGAIN!	WAITING FOR US IN A… LINE… HOW THEY… SHINE…
NOTHING'LL TURN LIFE UPSIDE-DOWN LIKE LUCK.	LIFE IS… FINE…
LUCK THAT'LL LAY YOU LOW OR TAKE YOU HIGH!	FOR ALL OUT TROUBLES ARE BEHIND…US

MAZEL.
>WHEN MAZEL SAYS HELLO.
>HER BLESSING SHE'LL BESTOW.

SHLIMAZEL.
>THEN UP SHLIMAZEL POPS
>AND TUMBLING DOWN YOUR FORTUNES GO!

PRINCESS.
>ISN'T A HAPPY ENDING GREAT?

TAM.
>HONEY, LET'S GO AND PROCREATE!

ALL.
>SAY WHAT YOU WILL, THERE'S NO DENYING
>LUCK IS WHY!
>LUCK!

(Curtain. End of show.)

OTHER TITLES AVAILABLE FROM SAMUEL FRENCH

PETE 'N' KEELY

Book by James Hindman
Original Music by Patrick Brady
Original Lyrics by Mark Waldrop, Patrick S, Brady and others

1m, 1f, 3 on stage musicians / Int.

Staged as a live taping of a 1968 television special that reunites a divorced singing duo, this kitschy spoof had New York critics singing its praises. As Pete and Keely stroll down memory lane (in eye popping costumes) reprising songs from their days of stardom, they take "unscripted" swipes at each other that dredge up hilarious moments from their turbulent past. This small scale musical from the director of When Pigs Fly and the producer of The Mystery of Irma Vep features unforgettable renditions of the era's popular favorites as well as original songs in the spirit of the times.

"Campy [with] nostalgic belly laughs."
– *The New York Times*

"A rattling good time.... The score is a mix of golden oldies, including a clever travelogue made of songs about every state in the Union, and silver newies.... A snappy scenario emerges ... [that] should leave no one unsmiling."
– *New York Magazine*

"The brightest, happiest, and most entertaining little show in town."
– New York Observer

"A sequined, bell bottomed parade of escalating fabulousness!"
– *Newsday*

www.ingramcontent.com/pod-product-compliance
Lightning Source LLC
Chambersburg PA
CBHW070639120726
47909CB00004B/1508